This is the thirteenth adventure in the bestselling "Contract" series by Philip Atlee, pseudonym of a Fayetteville, Arkansas, novelist of repute, and featuring government nullifier Joe Gall.

"Atlee's books are primarily to entertain. But he's too good a novelist to stop there. If you look carefully, you'll find—woven between the fact (he uses a real incident to build his story) and fiction—some well-thought-out gleanings of philosophy on today's world."

—*Southwest-Times Record*

OTHER FAWCETT GOLD MEDAL BOOKS
BY PHILIP ATLEE:

The Green Wound Contract
The Silken Baroness Contract
The Paper Pistol Contract
The Death Bird Contract
The Irish Beauty Contract
The Star Ruby Contract
The Rockabye Contract
The Skeleton Coast Contract
The Ill Wind Contract
The Trembling Earth Contract
The Fer-de-Lance Contract
The Canadian Bomber Contract

THE WHITE WOLVERINE CONTRACT

Philip Atlee

A FAWCETT GOLD MEDAL BOOK

Fawcett Publications, Inc., Greenwich, Conn.

THE WHITE WOLVERINE CONTRACT

Printed in the United States of America
December 1971

Man is the only animal with temerity enough to hunt the wolverine. All other predatory species found it dangerous and unprofitable long ago.

In deep snow, a forty-pound wolverine can attack and kill an adult bull moose weighing a ton. . . .

CHAPTER ONE

THE SIDEWALKS of downtown Vancouver were packed with hordes of fake Christs. These languid replicas were considerably dirtier than their prototype, and even in October most of them trudged barefooted through the spittle and slimy cigar butts. Their girl-women moved with them in tight jeans, faded tie-dyed shirts or blouses, and headbands.

Youth was the name of the hippie horde, although some of the unkempt dropouts were in their thirties or even forties. Most of them had drifted into Vancouver from the Unites States. Hitchhiking in with little or no funds and a back-pack of meager possessions, they had infested the back alleys and public conveniences of the beautiful Canadian seaport all summer.

Considering the fact that the hippie-lemmings had almost immediately become public charges, only a few trying for jobs where unemployment was already high, their unwilling hosts treated them with considerable restraint. A few muttered imprecations were to be heard when Vancouver residents stumbled over the hairy invaders as they huddled on stairways, lounged in busy doorways, and lay stoned and vacantly dreaming in public parks.

Now the indolent hippie beast was slouching, not toward Jerusalem, but Jericho. That was the name of the empty barracks at the city's outskirt to which they were being herded. The government of British Columbia had recently evicted them from a downtown arsenal where they slept until noon without segregation of the sexes, and openly turned on night and day with speed, hash, pot, and cocaine. No attempt had been made to conceal their drug use; indeed they flaunted it before reporters and were photographed for news broadcasts giggling, slack-mouthed, and firing off absurd demands that they be given a large amount of society's largess. *But not until noon, please, after they had awakened. . . .*

Many of them were psychotic, displayed severe personality disorders, and the rate of venereal infection was high and climbing. The few volunteer doctors and nurses who tried to combat it had no success because of the incidence of reinfection.

I knew all these facts because I had been sitting for two hours in the Mozart Konditorei on Robson Strasse with a Chinese girl named Kelly. (Of course her name wasn't Kelly. It was Miss Wu. And the Robson Strasse was really Robson Street, on Vancouver's glittering west side.)

Man cannot live by nomenclature alone. Miss Wu was Kelly because she had decided that would be a groovy thing for a healthy, shapely girl to call herself. The street was the Strasse because for blocks it featured specialty shops and stores selling European foods and products. German, Dutch, Austrian, Swiss: they were solid foreign enclaves in a city of many foreign colonies.

Not far away was a high-rise apartment building, the Johann Strauss, and a few blocks from that was the handsome new tower of the Rembrandt Hotel. As Kelly pointed these things out, I nodded and said it beat naming such structures after bankers or politicians.

"Watch, please!" Her hand touched my elbow, and I turned toward the direction her other slender hand was pointing. I didn't see anything interesting. Late afternoon traffic along Robson Strasse, with the employed worthies hurrying home and the hippies weaving through, around, and obstructing them. A sluice of one-way traffic toward North Vancouver featuring mostly European imports, an astonishing number of small Japanese cars including the Mazda (about which I had never heard), and many Jaguars and British sports cars. Occasionally, a Rolls purred by; many of these were waxed vintage models.

"So?" I asked. The Konditorei was a great little place for tea, crumpets, and *tortes,* but it had no license to serve beer or alcoholic drinks, and I was developing a dangerous bloat from tea and pastry.

"That postal box on the corner, by the Seamen's Institute," she commanded. "The red one. Every afternoon an unknown lady from one of the big luxury apartment towers comes down and leaves a foil-wrapped package, a big one, on top of the letter box. Tucked into it is a short, unsigned note asking that the package be taken as a gift by anyone who needs food."

I watched the red postal box on the next corner. There did seem to be an inordinate number of hippies pressing toward it. Casually, lounging past each other into doorways, inching toward the corner.

"It holds a fabulous meal, you see," Kelly rushed on, her dark eyes alive with excitement. "Caviar, smoked salmon and sturgeon, cheeses, biscuits. . . . Enough of a meal for several people, really."

When the Chinese girl said "really" it came out as "rally," and I mimicked her. She stuck out her tongue at me, and sat with her face cradled in both hands, waiting for the small miracle to arrive. Kelly Wu was about twenty-seven, tall for a Chinese girl. She moved often, and her breasts swung freely under the thin blouse when she did. They were obviously unconfined, and her dark skirt was short enough to show that she was wearing pantyhose.

"Oh, frig that," I said. "I'd rather look at your legs."

Her face, still cradled in her hands, turned to survey me briefly. "Your remark, with its Freudian implications in the first phrase, is not really the thing, Mr. Gardner."

She angled her head to the other side and thrust her shapely legs into full view. The modish shoes had blunt toes, and she waggled them.

"They aren't bad, are they?" she asked. "Still, I must ask you not to be such a toilet-mouthed Yank, in my presence."

"Right," I said, getting up. "Pardon."

I walked back through the crowded tables topped by spotless napery to the can. While my distended bladder was discharging oolong, I wondered how long this badinage was going to last. Kelly Wu was the secretary of J.

Donald Atwater, a Vancouver alderman and millionaire real estate man. Her employer was a showboat of the highest order, according to report, and would rather be dead than out of the public eye.

J. Donald Atwater was what the news photographers call a "lens louse." At the recent dedication of a huge tower being built in the center of Vancouver, he had upstaged the mayor by leaping out onto the final girder while it was being swung into place, on the twenty-eighth floor. Actually riding the damned thing as it was craned and bolted into place. The rest of the dedication party had been completely forgotten while the photographers shot J. Donald, gripping the swinging steel beam on all fours. . . .

So, an eccentric: every government has them. The difference was that J. Donald Atwater, a Canadian born in British Columbia, had for years been a bristling supporter of the theory that his province should voluntarily withdraw from the Canadian Federal Union and join the United States of America. For most of these years this treasonous suggestion had been ignored because he was a powerhouse in municipal good works. The Vancouver press reported his antics faithfully, if often with tongue in cheek, as a valuable civic leader. It was this odd predilection of his, British Columbia's union with the States, which had brought me to Vancouver.

The idea that British Columbia should become one of the United States is not held by even a strong minority of that province's citizens, but those who champion the cause are highly vocal. The west coast of Canada came late to unity with the prairie and eastern provinces, and many people in British Columbia honestly feel that their section has long been slighted by Ontario and Quebec. And in the past few decades, many U.S. ranchers have removed to the upland caribou ranges and many Yank businessmen to Vancouver and Victoria.

As in all the rest of Canada, the dominant economic force comes from below the border. A majority interest in nearly all large businesses is owned by U.S. corporations. Add to these factors the social pressure of a severe recession in the province and the flocking in of hippies and *métis* seeking the balmy climate, and you have a specious but enthusiastic nucleus for separation from the federal union centered in Ottawa.

As I stared at my lean visage in the mirror, regretting the ravages of time and the scar tissue, I could still not help admiring the essential mobility of the reflected face. That wide brow could have encompassed any thought.

Actually, while I dried my hands on the virgin towel I was wondering, if I played my tarot cards just right, whether or not I could peel the blunt-toed shoes and beige pantyhose off Miss Wu. . . .

I wound my way back through the Konditorei tables, and found Kelly jabbing her fingers again. Still at the postal box on the far corner. There *was* an aluminum-foil-wrapped package on it, and hippies began to materialize out of doorways, alleys, and across the Robo-Wash parking lot.

Some of them were openly hurrying toward the red mail box when a door opened suddenly in a saloon across the street. From the licensed premises late afternoon bar drinkers broke across the street on the dead run. There were young clerks among them, laboring men in dirty coveralls, and cab drivers with caps askew on their heads.

The men streaming from the bar were racing the hippies to the free meal on the postal box. Seeing their intention, the hairy ones gave up the pretense that they just happened to be in the neighborhood. They bolted forward, and the two dissident streams of running people collided. A small riot erupted.

A young man in mod attire, one of the first out of the saloon door, captured the prize. Lifted the foil-wrapped package and danced around, holding it aloft. Whirling.

When the wave hit him, he threw the food to the curb with great ostentation, and began stomping on it with his fashionable boots. Slowly, the battle was unjoined. The milling individual battles came to a halt, and the hungry hippies stared at their more affluent opponents. Angry words were exchanged, but these trailed off, too. The defenders of the system retreated, laughing, into the bar again.

A few irresolute hippies stood staring at the rich food

stomped into pulp, but after a few cars had whirled it around, they trudged away.

At the table beside me, Kelly Wu unleashed a string of quiet oaths which would have made a logger or a mule-skinner nod with appreciation.

"All they did," she said, simmering down, "was destroy a meal for several people." I didn't answer, and the slanted eyes swung on me over an outraged, full mouth. "And you belong to the same club."

I shrugged, *"Mas o menos.* Look, can't we go wait somewhere else? I mean, where we can get a drink? These *tortes* are killing me."

"No," she answered coldly, "Mr. Atwater told us to wait here for a message, and that's what we'll do. I'm on overtime, too, you know."

"Yes, of course." An hour before, J. Donald Atwater had delivered another inflammatory speech to his colleagues in the Vancouver municipal government. This one, however, was wilder than most; he had called for a plebiscite in British Columbia, to decide on immediate secession from the Canadian Federal Government, in order to petition for entrance into the United States. As its fifty-first state. If successfully concluded, this act would have given the U.S. an unbroken Pacific shoreline from Alaska to Mexico, and would add rich and almost untapped mineral treasures to our Yank domain.

Kelly Wu went to the can, threading her way through the tables like a ballerina.

Alderman Atwater had staked Kelly Wu and me out in this teahouse to monitor his actions after he delivered the speech. He might be justified in his fear of danger. Neal Pearsall, head of the agency's action division, had sent me in on short notice.

Robson Strasse was darkening beyond the glass windows. Kelly Wu came flouncing back, settled herself with a good deal more show of pantyhose than was necessary, and smiled at me. We ordered more tea.

From our streetside table, we could see the tremendous bloom of night jewelry, across Burrard Inlet on the far shores. The fine harbor went from glinting black water to a ring of twinkling slopes, and the thin line of lights snaking up the far mountain to the Grouse Mountain cable car. The bridge span sparkled; unseen now beyond the Lion's Gate were the peaks which gave it a name . . .

"What will J. Donald be doing now?" I asked.

"Oh . . ." She glanced at her watch. "He'll have had dinner, after three martinis. His wife will be cautioning him to put on another sweater before he takes his walk . . ."

"Oh?"

"Yes, Mr. Gardner."

"What are we supposed to be waiting for?"

"He thinks he will be hurt, tonight, because of the speech."

"So we have to spend our lives here, waiting to hear if he got low-bridged for his opinions?"

"Well . . ." She hesitated. "We might wait in my apartment."

"Let's do that."

When I had attracted the attention of the waitress, I paid the bill, and Kelly Wu and I went out onto Robson and caught a cab. She had a lovely apartment, and I sipped cognac while she vanished into its bathroom. At my elbow on the coffee table was an opened small carton of cigarillos, Willem twos, made in Holland. I tried one.

Kelly came back in a thin robe. She stopped before me, and I picked her up and was carrying her into the darkened bedroom when the telephone began ringing. . . .

CHAPTER TWO

"YES?" The tall Chinese girl listened, one arm held over her bared breasts. Her dark hair was tousled. While I watched, her lips flattened, and she said "Oh, no!" Then listened again.

Kelly cradled the phone, snatched at some clothes, and as she went toward the bathroom said that the caller had been Rachel Atwater, the alderman's wife. Atwater had been severely beaten, bound, and tossed into the sea in Eagle Harbor. He was now on his way to the emergency ward of St. Paul's Hospital.

"Jesus," I commented, lighting another of the little Dutch cigars. "They pay off fast around here."

Kelly came out of the bathroom wearing black pants, a dark cashmere sweater, and a rakish, flat-brimmed matador's hat. When I began to hum "Lady of Spain, I Adore You," she shook her head and said that my geography was pretty crazy. But the impish lightness was gone.

We got a cab, went wheeling down Robson, and turned right toward Burrard and the old hospital. A police guard at the emergency ward door barred me, but Kelly said I was with her, so he waved me by. There were no patients in sight, no activity at all in the bleak room smelling of blood, urine, and disinfectants. Kelly found a nurse down the hall, and she reported that Alderman Atwater had just been taken up to surgery.

We went up to the fourth floor and found more police guards. This time they were RCMPs, and denied both of us entry. When Kelly explained who she was, and produced identification, they suggested that she go around to the gallery. St. Paul's was a teaching hospital, and had an observation gallery above the main surgical room. We walked around to its entrance, Kelly explained again, saying that I was an American associate of Alderman Atwater, and we were admitted.

The subject of this close guard was on the table, and had already been draped. The surgical field was on the right side of the head, above the ear, which was matted with dried blood. What we could see of Atwater's face was waxen pale. The anesthesiologist had already put him under, and was checking his cylinders and insufflator bladder. The instrument nurse was waiting at her station, but the surgical team had not come in from scrubbing.

The oval observation gallery hung close to the surgical table, but was about nine feet above the floor below. Four reporters were waiting with us, but photographers had been barred. In addition, there were several men in suits whom I took to be doctors, three young interns in rumpled white work clothes, and two nurses.

Kelly Wu, the chic Spanish matador, walked over to one of the interns and asked him how badly Atwater was hurt.

"We're not sure, Miss. That's why we've got him up here. Somebody pounded him around the head pretty good, I know that much, because I was on duty in Emergency when they brought him in. There's one definite skull fracture just above the right hairline. . . ."

I moved over to one of the reporters, and asked him what had happened to the Alderman. He had been scribbling in a notebook, and glanced up with disinterested eyes.

"You are?" he inquired.

I said that I was a business associate of Atwater, and showed him my phony U.S. passport in the name of Gardner. Added that Miss Wu, the Alderman's secretary, would vouch for me.

"Hey, Kelly!" shouted the reporter. "You know this Yank?"

The Chinese girl was still talking to the intern, but she turned and nodded. The reporter flipped back through his notebook and gave me what he had, speaking without emphasis.

"After delivering another of his pro-American speeches before this afternoon's council meeting, Atwater went to his office, then to his home. West side of Vancouver, above Eagle Harbor. Had dinner at six o'clock then took his red Irish setter down to the beach for a stroll.

"Walked about a half mile. When turning back, was set upon by persons unknown, beaten viciously, and when unconscious was bound and a jute bag put over his head and wired around his throat. If they had waited another twenty minutes, the assailants would not have been seen. Twilight was nearly full, but a police guard stationed above the beach saw the altercation and ran down toward it.

"The attackers saw him coming and splashed through the surf to board a waiting launch. The guard fished J. Donald Atwater out of the water, but was hampered by his pedigreed setter, which had done absolutely nothing while his master was being kicked and hammered senseless by strangers. So much for good breeding, and man's best friend.

"At 7:21 P.M., Atwater was loaded into an ambulance and driven to St. Paul's Hospital. The jute sack, when removed, was found to be stitched on both sides and tied at the upper corners. On it were faded letters resembling 'HPS-38/41 VANCOUVER', with a diamond containing the numeral '4' underneath. . . ."

The reporter broke off, closing his notebook. "That's it, chum. Here come the butchers."

The three-man surgical team, gowned in light green and rubber gloved, was entering the surgical theatre below us, followed by the scrub nurse. The battery of brilliant lights over the figure on the table flared on.

"Thanks," I whispered to the reporter, and he nodded.

"Nothing. Just remember you got it first from the *Province*."

I moved back to join the tall Chinese girl, who was still chatting with the intern. In fact, I had to rip her out of his area, because, as he openly stated, death and disease were things he spent most of his time with. Miss Wu . . . Kelly could have stood tons of this stuff, but I removed her to a place apart and we sat staring down.

While I had been talking to the reporter, someone had

shaved all the hair off Atwater's skull on the right side. That area was stained bright orange. The blood had been removed from his ear. The chief surgeon held out his right gloved hand for an instrument, and it was slapped into his palm. He was staring across the table at the X rays banked across the mobile fluoroscope panel. Murmuring something we could not hear through his mask to the surgeon assisting, he opened up the head with a deft stroke of the scalpel.

As if on cue, a monstrous disturbance began behind him. Out of sight, back beyond the scrub room. A man's voice, first, angry shouts, then a nurse's higher-pitched outcry, demanding that—both protests were stilled abruptly by a stuttering fusillade which I knew had come from a carbine, firing full automatic.

Three men dressed in rough work clothes and wearing ski masks came bursting into the surgical theatre. The one in front cautioned the astonished doctors and nurses away from the table by jerky motions from his leveled carbine. The other two dragged the unconscious patient off the operating table to the floor, and began kicking him around methodically with steel-toed logger's boots. The carbine-wielder kept backing the surgical team away, circling, until he had them against the far wall.

This maneuver left him almost below us, below the rim of the viewing gallery, and I thought that they must not have researched the job very well. No one came up the stairs to guard us; the intruders below were acting as if they did not even know about the observation gallery.

Reaction time had been slow. But, thank God, no one shouted or panicked. My informative friend, the reporter from the *Province,* had tiptoed out quietly, and the rest of them had gotten up and pressed backward, to get out of any possible line of fire. All except Miss Kelly Wu. I pushed down hard on her shoulder, getting up, and put a warning finger to my lips.

I went down the two steps to the edge of the observation gallery and moved right until I was directly over the fellow brandishing the carbine. As I vaulted over the short brass railing polished by generations of attentive medical students, I could hear the bone-breaking kicks being delivered to Alderman Atwater's limp body.

I dropped feet-first, with legs slightly spread, so that the full weight of my body was distributed through them to the shoulders of the carbine-holder. When I thudded into him, I caromed off to one side, scrambled up, and lunged for the carbine. He was down and groaning, both shoulders broken, knocked out of place.

The other two ski-masked intruders who had been kicking Atwater turned in surprise, and I tried to trigger a burst at them. Nothing happened; I had damaged the weapon on my precipitate drop onto its holder. They rushed me. I reversed the weapon and used its stock as a flail, clubbing the first one to his knees. The other one turned and ran like a deer, and I was lunging for him when his floored assistant grabbed at my legs.

He paid for the one who had escaped. As he clawed and punched I clubbed him with the carbine stock until it was bloodied. He went flat under my blows with the reversed weapon, and was rousing when I smashed him so hard that the carbine came apart in my hands.

Then I lifted the bleeding body of Alderman J. Donald Atwater and put it back on the operating table. When that was done, I walked into the scrub room and vomited into the sink.

CHAPTER THREE

KELLY WU, the surgical team, and the reporters came crowding into the scrub room. I was not glad to see any of them, because I was still on the high wire, trembling with rage. An impromptu news conference was held on the second floor, in the office of the hospital's Medical Director, Dr. Frank Cost. (I had told him I would agree to it if there were no photographers.)

Dr. Cost looked like Pasteur after a failed experiment. He had a white beard, and a nose prominent enough to run for public office. He put great stress on the fact that one of our Yank friends had reacted so bravely and immediately. The carbine-wielding intruder had two broken clavicles, he announced jocularly, and would not soon again menace decent society, much less invade the sanctity of the operating theater.

Called upon to say a few words, I stated that I had noticed that the intruder carrying the carbine had been vulnerable, because he was directly below our part of the observation gallery, and seemed not to know it was there. That I had been appalled by the onslaught against the patient, and had interrupted it through sheer reflex action.

The conference was dissolving when an intern brought a message to Dr. Cost. Alderman Atwater had just died of his wounds. The charge against the intruder with the broken shoulders, his still unconscious associate, and the escaped man, therefore, was noncapital murder.

After a lot of nattering, the crowd drifted out of Cost's office. Some of the reporters asked for pictures; their photographers were waiting in front of the hospital. I said no. One of them wanted to do a feature story on the brave

Yank who had vaulted the balcony and interrupted the intruders. I said no. During most of this, Kelly Wu was standing at my elbow. When the entreaters had gone out, she asked if I would be spending the night in her apartment. I said no, and she went flouncing out with her hips-akimbo model walk.

When she was gone, there was no one left in the Medical Director's office but the surly reporter clod who had given me the information upstairs. He was sitting in a chair tilted back against the wall. A completely relaxed cat with thick sideburns down to his jawline.

"Okay," he said. "You're pretty cute. There's not a businessman alive who could have figured the situation out that fast, and stopped it. So the reports are true. Your agency has moved into Vancouver."

He was perhaps twenty-five, or twenty-six years old, and he knew nothing. But, like all good reporters, he smelled something and was not willing to let it go.

"Man," I said, "My passport proves what I am. There are certain things I can tell the press. If you want to have an original source, give me your card."

He snorted, "Who has cards?" But he scribbled something on his notebook, tore out the page, and handed it to me. "Home telephone, too."

"Thanks," I said, and went walking down the echoing corridor. The muted address system was paging doctors, and I thought that it was the same in every hospital I had ever been in. Where, I wondered, do all those sawbones get off to?

CHAPTER FOUR

AT THE ENTRANCE to the hospital, I told the RCMP constable stationed there that I would like to speak to the ranking mountie official on duty. He asked politely after the nature of my business, and when I said I could not divulge it, turned to the house phone inside the hospital door. In a few minutes, a plainclothes RCMP officer showed up, from inside the place somewhere.

He wanted to know the nature of my business too, but didn't get it. After eyeing me speculatively, he inquired if I was not the gentleman who had crippled two of the intruders. I admitted I was, and he scribbled something on a piece of paper and said that it was the address of RCMP headquarters. The duty officer there would be glad to assist me in any way he could.

"Not good enough," I said. "I have an Ottawa telephone number here. If I pay for the call, would you please read my name and passport number off this, forwarding my request?"

He studied my gray-green U.S. passport, with its number perforated through the top of the front cover. Noted the date of issue, only ten days ago.

"No, sir, I am not empowered to do that," he said. "Nothing to do with you, understand, just money passing hands. I can, however, put the message on our direct telex to Ottawa, and they can phone from there. No charge, but might take an hour to get an answer."

"I'd appreciate it," I said, and went to sit in the hospital lobby. The constable guarding the door was still checking everyone who entered or left, and between these chores he kept glancing at me curiously. In forty minutes, the plainclothes mountie came back and informed me that Royal Canadian Mounted Police Provincial Assistant Commissioner Henning would see me in an hour, at headquarters. The plainclothesman was curious, and puzzled by the speed with which the message had round-tripped.

There was nothing surprising about it. The government in Ottawa had been consulted beforehand when Williamson, our earlier agent, had been sent in, and my presence was also known to them.

I walked out of the hospital and got a sandwich and beer in the Red Lion Inn's licensed premises. The sandwich was terrible, and I told the burly waiter so. That was a mistake; as he sucked loudly at his upper teeth and considered me sadly, I noticed for the first time he was loaded.

"I expect, sir, that we're not posh enough for you here. I take the liberty to suggest that you walk on down to the Hotel Victoria and get a dish of hummingbird's bums. . . ."

I nodded, without speaking, dropped a tip on the table, and went to pay my bill. My fault: because of the dim light in the joint, I had not noticed that the waiter was swaying around on his ankles. In the brief time I had been in Vancouver, I had first noticed the spectacular beauty of the Pacific Coast port, then the tremendous variety of its shops and stores, and had only belatedly noted the high incidence of its eccentrics, crackpots and alcoholics.

Whenever you build a city of a million people, with an international range of ethnic origins, you are bound to come up with a large number of oddballs. Vancouver, it seemed to me, abused the franchise. You expect seamen ashore, loggers out on the town, and oil-drilling crews on a weekend sabbatical to get drunk, brawl, and generally rip up the pea patch.

Vancouver went far beyond this expectance. All day, its triangular Pigeon Park was covered with passed-out drunks. As you walked by its smart shops, in the best sections of town, you encountered men in business suits who were hurrying along, seemingly quite normal. Suddenly they would lurch out of gear and you realized they were soused to the gills. Two days before, I had been riding on a city bus when a well dressed, patriarchal old man with a white beard had leaned over to tap me on the knee.

"Get out of town, boy!" he admonished me in ringing tones.

"Why?" I had asked.

"Witchcraft. Everywhere. Casting spells, the bastards are. . . ."

I nodded, and said I was planning to leave soon. The patriarch looked like a Scottish laird, and he nodded his white mane vigorously, in approval. But when he got up to leave the bus, a few blocks further on, he was unable to operate the swinging panel which opened the back door, and had to be helped off. No one in the crowded bus even noticed, except for the laughing workingman who helped him off.

The assistant commissioner of the RCMP, G. C. Henning, was waiting in his office when I arrived at mountie headquarters. He was a tall, balding man with a conventional reddish moustache going gray. I asked if he knew about my participation in foiling the attack on Alderman Atwater, and he nodded. Then I said that I would like to see the exhibits connected with the late alderman's beach attack.

"Right. Let's go down here, shall we?" Henning, ramrod stiff, led the way out of the large paneled office and down the hall to a counter in a larger room. The clerk-constable on duty there nodded when Henning said he wanted the Atwater evidence, and placed a large plywood file box on the counter. The assistant commissioner unloaded the box by turning it over.

"Have a go," he said mildly, but without enthusiasm. I suspected that he had been enjoying a drink or bridge game at home when Ottawa had ordered him to go back down to the office and humor the bloody Yank.

The jute sack which had been wired over the late alderman's head was still damp. The foot-long copper strand which had secured it was also there. Two frayed strands of rope which had bound his hands and ankles. . . . I picked the jute sack up: it was, as the reporter from the *Province* had told me, stitched down both sides and tied at the upper corners, with what seemed binder's twine. The letters and numbers he had mentioned were faded on the rough sack, but you could make them out.

As I looked the things over, I had been replacing them in the plywood file box. Now there was only one object left on the counter. It was a carved figurine of an animal, about an inch long, with a supple metal chain and a wicked-looking little barbed hook protruding from its back. The figurine seemed hand carved, and represented a chunky, weasellike figure, with a bearlike head. The punisher's jaw was opened to show formidable fangs.

"Wolverine?" I asked, and Henning nodded. "And the material?"

"Walrus ivory," he said curtly.

"Handmade?"

"Yes."

"A white one. Do albino wolverines occur?"

"Yes."

"Where was this one found?"

The assistant commissioner ran a weathered hand over his graying moustache. "The barb had been run through the right earlobe of Alderman Atwater. It had to be removed surgically."

"Do you have any idea why it was placed there?"

"None at all, sir. This case is the first time we have seen such a figurine, whether or not in connection with a criminal case. At least in this province."

An eardrop on an intended corpse. . . . And for a subject, the sculptor had chosen the elusive predator, the most ferocious member of the *mustelid* family, which regularly raided Canadian traplines and caches, but was almost never, itself, caught in a trap. On the rare occasions when it was, the wolverine chewed off its trapped leg and often survived to hunt on, using three legs. If its lair were threatened, the animal would attack man. In deep snow, a forty-pound wolverine could hamstring and kill an adult bull moose weiging a ton. . . .

I weighed the little figurine in my right hand, and noted the dried blood on the barbed tip.

"You have never seen, Commissioner, a duplicate of this one?" I asked.

Henning shook his head. "No. Harry, have you?"

The clerk shook his head.

"Could I, with proper arrangements, have the figurine for a few days?"

"No, sir." The graying moustache was almost quivering. "It is a part of the evidence against the ruffian whose shoulders you broke tonight. The other fellow, and his mate, when we apprehend him."

I nodded, smiling at his phraseology. *When* we apprehend them, not *if*. The idea went through my mind that the Royal Canadian Mounted Police might have a lot in common with our own Federal Bureau of Investigation.

"Then I'll say goodnight, sir, and thanks."

"Right." Assistant Commissioner Henning nodded. "If you need any other assistance, this office will be happy to provide it. Now, if you'll excuse me, I'll be off."

He stalked off down the hall with a grenadier's back, turned into his office, and came back out immediately, shrugging into a topcoat and pulling on gloves. The man on duty came to attention and saluted as he left the building.

"Pissed off, isn't he?" I asked Harry. This worthy was putting the Atwater evidence box back on its rack, and he snickered.

"Well, sir, you might say that," he admitted. "Mr. Henning rarely comes back down to the office at night. You put your message through to Ottawa, and he got a rocket at home. Stirred him up, of course."

Harry was a bandy man with bowed legs and an Irish lilt. I count both of these things as assets, since I come from a long line of bog-trotters. When I asked him where the best place to check such handmade figurines as the snarling wolverine carved from walrus ivory might be, he wrote down the names of three Vancouver native-art shops. He was sure that I would not find figurines like the one which had pierced Atwater's ear in the cheaper tourist bazaars.

I thanked him, saying that I hoped he would always be held in the palm of God's hand, and he grinned.

"Thank you, Yank," he said. "Up the Irish, eh?"

It was raining outside, and I didn't know whether or not

the buses were still running. So I struck out toward my high-rise apartment building, only nine or ten blocks away. Before I got there, bedraggled hippies darted at me four times, out of doorways, begging. Four times I quartered them off, and the last importuner, a soaked girl in a poncho, cursed me for a mother-jumping miser, *after* she had her quarter.

The apartment lobby was empty when I ducked into it out of the driving rain. Went up to the fifteenth floor, and stood staring at the door to my apartment. The strip of adhesive I had left across the lock was gone, although I had told the management I did not want any maid service after 6 P.M. Somebody else had entered.

Easing the key into the lock, I turned it slowly, and slipped inside. There were no lights in the apartment except in the bedroom. I moved cautiously toward it, and saw Miss Kelly Wu enthroned in the center of my bed. She was reading *Georgia Straight,* the Vancouver underground newspaper. On the bedside table was a carton of ice cubes, several glasses, and a dish of lime quarters. Most prominent was a bottle of Martel Cordon Bleu cognac.

"Got the freeze treatment over at mountie headquarters, didn't you?" she asked. Her jet hair was down, in two pigtails.

"Something like that," I admitted, advancing into the bedroom and shrugging out of the sodden raincoat. While I was hanging it up in the closet, I asked what she was doing in my bed.

Kelly blinked behind her huge oval glasses, purple tinted, and tried to recapture the light air. But it didn't work. She began to weep, holding both hands to her mouth, and the ridiculous glasses fell off.

"I didn't even like him," she sobbed, "but nobody should die like that."

"Not your fault." I went over, kissed her upright, and said she was not to worry. After I had showered, we would go get a pizza with everything on it. Okay?

"Yes, please."

I had the shower, and changed into freshly laundered socks, underwear, and shirt while she watched.

"What I really am is frightened," she said. "After we eat, can I spend the night here?"

"If you like," I said. She threw off the covers and ran naked into the bathroom. While I was shaving, trying to keep the mirror free from the steam she was generating behind the shower curtain, Kelly Wu was belting out "Lady of Spain," and I thought the song traveled well.

CHAPTER FIVE

TEN DAYS BEFORE, I had been sitting in a jetliner when it landed on the Victoria International Airport. Victoria, the capital of British Columbia, is a lovely garden city at the southern tip of Vancouver Island. Because many people had told me that it was the finest place to live on the North American continent, I was curious. The area around the airport was not impressive, and the airport bus rolled toward the city on a potholed road which was being widened.

The entrance to the city itself was no more prepossessing: the usual Los Angeles-type of commercial litter on both sides. As we neared the center of Victoria, things improved. An interesting mall of shops, an old but well-kept city hall, and a few blocks further on a huge red brick church squarely on the main drag. The bus stopped behind the car park of the Empress Hotel, an enormous, sprawling pile of gray stone covered with ivy.

From the front, the Empress has the finest location of any hotel in the world. Behind wide and immaculate lawns and flower beds, it dominates the city's Inner Harbor. The interior halls are so wide you could run railroads through them, and on its acres of roof the copper capping has weathered to a pale green. To the south and southwest of the Empress, separted from the harbor only by lengendary Government Street, are the parliament buildings of British Columbia. These structures are immense, pillared, and rooted in meticulously tended lawns.

Surveying that view, I began to realize that there might be more than propaganda to Victoria's claims. When I had claimed my one bag, I walked south up Douglas Street to the slope which held Thunderbird Park. This small corner park was a thicket of huge totems; some of the poles of red cedar seemed sixty feet high. The figures carved on them were boldly done and vividly painted. Eagles, bears, ravens . . . the only human figures represented seemed to be children.

That was natural enough, since the totems were never objects of religious veneration but coats-of-arms for a large Indian family, or tribe. Haida, the bear-mother, seemed to appear on most of the poles. Now, in late afternoon, the sun gone westering over the Pacific sent long shadows through the totem forest, striping the emerald lawn.

Putting my bag down on a bench, I sat beside it, lighted a small cigar, and began my vigil on the conservatory which was the rear entrance to the Empress. The greenhouse itself was old, oblong, and the greenery inside it nearly obscured by whitewashed panes. A covered walk came down from it into the car park, and that was another desecration. An asphalt acre covered by gas-hog polluting machines.

A hotel like the Empress should have beech-shaded drives winding to all its entrances, with teams of matched grays spinning the wheels of sparkling landaus. . . .

I smiled grimly at this thought, because it was like wanting to take flying lessons from Leonardo da Vinci. My real name is Joseph Liam Gall, and I am a contract counterespionage agent for a large U.S. agency. I have been that for a good many years, and have served my country as a back-alley brigand in many parts of the world.

I was not always proud of what I did, during those years, but as a stopper, who got most of the dirty cases when they were almost beyond saving, I was good at the job. It paid highly, and for me was a better way of earning a living than smiling at people I did not like, as insurance salesmen and used-car dealers do.

It also allowed me to live in a large clapboard castle on top of a remote Ozarks Mountain hill. A hundred-odd acres of pine, and spring-fed streams, surrounded the eyrie I had restored, and the estate was enclosed by an electrified fence. When I was not out on contract, it was my world, complete with waterfall, an Edo-period garden fringed by clumps of black bamboo, a *dojo* gym, and mushroom-cultivation caves in the cellar.

The assignment which had brought me to Victoria, on Vancouver Island, was unusual. By contract, I had the right to consider a potential assignment for twenty-four hours, although I had seldom done so. The normal procedure was for an agency courier to fly to St. Louis, rent a car, and drive down to my high eyrie. I then read the dossiers and other relevant material the courier had in the attaché case chained to his wrist, and decided while he waited.

On this one, the courier had come without any details, or even general instructions. He had buzzed my house from the electrified gate down the hill, and after viewing him on the television intercom screen in my pantry, I had buzzed him through. He had no attaché case, but showed me a sheaf of plane tickets and said that Neal Pearsall was jammed up and wanted me in Victoria the next afternoon.

It was a blind assignment, and I could take it or leave it. Since Pearsall was head of the agency's action division, and my boss when I worked, the instructions were so precipitate that I had stared at the courier. At our last meeting, Pearsall and I had had our first serious argument in all the years I had worked for him. I wondered if he was invoking a rush clause, with no definition, to provoke me into a refusal and thus terminate my agency employment.

Pearsall was a friend of mine, or had been, but he was a better friend of the United States. His whole life, every working hour, was dedicated to the agency. His marriage had foundered on that single-mindedness. As a Marine major in Korea, he had lost his right leg from gangrene after chivying his troops out of an ambush, and he was a fine man for his sensitive job, protecting his agents in the field. But he would not tolerate even the slightest implication that the agency was ever wrong, in any degree.

I took the courier into my living room, with the fourteen-foot beamed ceilings, and set him out a tray containing a bottle of J & B Scotch, a silver bucket of ice, and a carafe of chilled spring water. Telling him he was free to raid the refrigerator for cold turkey, or whatever else he could find.

The courier was young: most of them were. If they were any good, they went up fast, in the agency.

"Jesus, Mr. Gall," he said, staring around the huge room at the molten log, collapsing in the twelve-foot fireplace. "This place looks like a miniature cathedral."

I smiled, because it did. The Gothic stained-glass windows, the high ceilings, and the carved walnut paneling on the walls.

"A carpetbagger Union General built it, just after the Civil War. Name of Powell Clayton. No relation, so I'm told, to the Harlem Congressman of the same reversed name. Anyway he had a pipe organ down at the other end of the room."

I went upstairs and packed a bag, resentful because Neal had given me no time to shut the huge house down properly. There were things growing in my greenhouse which needed constant attention. There was food which would spoil, especially in the walk-in refrigerator down in the basement. Since I had to consider every trip for the agency my last one, until that thesis was disproved I would have to use the Swedish woman in Tulsa, the only one I trusted, to drive over and spend two days shutting the tempo of the clapboard castle down.

In an hour we were rolling toward Tulsa in the courier's rented car. At the airport he took my keys and my sealed instructions for Mrs. Lundquist, and I flew to Kansas City. There I caught a direct flight to Seattle, and the next afternoon was flying into Victoria.

CHAPTER SIX

MY INSTRUCTIONS were to wait on the bench in Thunderbird Park until 6:45 P.M., Pacific time. An agency representative would walk out of the conservatory door in the rear of the Empress Hotel, cross the car park, and enter the Royal London Wax Museum. This building was across the street from the car park, and adjacent to the Crystal Palace swimming pool, which was also ivy-covered, and which featured terraces of potted plants and light teas.

My plane had been on time; I sat looking toward the Empress' conservatory entrance through the fading light. I had not been told who the agency representative would be, but when he came out from the covered steps I recognized him immediately. A big, bulky man wearing expensive clothes, well rumpled, hitching slightly in his gait, modish furled umbrella hooked over his right forearm and a dark felt hat on his head.

Neal Pearsall. The director of the action division had thought the assignment important enough to come in person. I watched him cross the car park, the street, and, whirling his bumbershoot, enter the Royal London Wax Museum. I waited ten minutes, got off the bench, and walked down the slope of Douglas Street to approach its box office.

After paying the fee, I walked down the narrow, darkened aisle between the exhibits of life-sized waxen figurines. All authenticated by Madame Tussaud. The exhibits were divided into glass-fronted sections, the figures artfully lighted, and recorded tapes constantly replayed appropriate theme music or comment. Not many of the wax figures were good likenesses, but the backgrounds were well done. Queen Victoria, perhaps in honor of the city, was almost alive, although Disraeli was just a dummy.

Most of them missed a real likeness, but in the dimly lighted corridors, with artful lighting and muted noises, it didn't make much difference. Abe Lincoln had been cruelly used; he was so gaunt and shadow-eyed that he looked like a corpse. The best figure Madame Tussaud had sent this outpost of Empire was a receptionist behind a ticket grill, a young girl in modern dress. If she had winked an eye, I'd have invited her out for coffee.

Neal Pearsall was waiting up ahead, leaning on his fashionable umbrella. Even in the dim light, I could see he was wearing an Irish hacking jacket that must have cost $200.

"Pardon me," I said, stopping behind him. "What time does the next fox leave?"

"Joseph," he sighed, not looking at me, "when will you learn respect for your elders?"

"I'm sorry, Your Gimpiness, I forgot that you were a year and two months older than I am."

"Not quite relevant," he said. "Now stare at the exhibit and keep quiet until the museum is empty."

"Stays open until nine tonight," I informed him.

"Not now," he answered. "I have bought it out for an hour."

"Okay." I watched the exhibit. It was called the Algerian Hook, and showed an Arab with both ends of his body sagging in despair. Which was understandable because he was impaled through the middle back by a huge hook. To the right below him, on a rude bench, was a hook victim who had not made it, coated with congealed gore.

Every few seconds, anguished groans came off the tape behind the glass-plated barbarity. Several tourists came crowding behind us, were properly horrified, and drifted on down the dim-lighted aisle.

Neal was annoyed. "Go back and see if that stupid girl is still selling tickets. I paid them enough to shut the joint down and go home."

I reversed my way down the shadowed path to the languid girl at the cash register. She wore blue-green eyeshadow and had fat thighs, plainly visible.

"Are you still selling tickets?" I asked.
"Only a few," she simpered at me.
"Well, don't. No more. Or I'll throw that cash register out into the street, probably breaking it. You will follow, but you're too fat to break. When you get paid to do something, do it."
"Yes. Yes . . ." She started punching the machine, and went out to hang a closed sign on the waxworks museum. "Only an hour, mind!"
I turned back down the dark corridor with the garbled recorded groans and muted dialogue. The second time through, Bach seemed lifelike enough to talk to, but unfortunately, I know little about music. Neal Pearsall was still leaning on the handle of his umbrella cane, and when I stopped behind him he did not turn.
"Joseph," he said, "the last time we met, in the horse country of Virginia, we had a misunderstanding. It was mostly my fault, and I apologize for it."
I was not ready for anything like that. "Not necessary, Neal. I was out of line, edgy from a tough assignment. A man can have private loyalties, and I picked a bad time to bring up one of mine."
My suggestion had been that Neal use his influence to have the agency propose a general amnesty for all draft dodgers and deserters from the Vietnam war. This as a necessary concomitant to any end to the war there. In my suggestion, I had emphasized that those who had actually committed criminal acts would be barred from such an amnesty, but that the United States could ill afford to lose the others, those who had made an important, life-shattering moral decision, a thing which most American citizens live out their whole lives without doing.
"Okay," growled Pearsall, his back still to me. "That was some time ago, and I hope we're still friends."
"More than that. If you knew there was a machine-gun emplacement with a full traverse waiting for me in the Empress car park, and you told me to silence it—"
"Joseph," said Neal Pearsall, "you're a rotten bastard. Will you listen?"
"Yes, sir."

CHAPTER SEVEN

WHILE PEARSALL was outlining the problem, I stared at the unfortunate with the Algerian Hook in his back. Above and behind us along the narrow aisles of the Wax Museum, recorded sound effects kept playing over and over. . . .

Neal said that for five months persistent reports had been reaching Washington that our agency was deeply involved in a British Columbia operation. The supposed reason for such clandestine action by us was to promote a breakaway faction in British Columbia which favored union with the United States.

He said that the carefully planted rumors were absolute crap. The agency had routed men through Vancouver and Victoria, but had never maintained an agent in either city, or anywhere else in British Columbia. Still, he had been curious about the reason for it, other than making Uncle Sam the black dog, as usual. . . .

"This business of a union between B.C. and the States has historical precedent, Joseph. In 1870, General Grant was presented with a memorandum signed by many property-owners and businessmen of British Columbia, suggesting that the American President propose negotiations for such a switch in fealty to the British Crown. Grant, in turn, promised to lay the matter before his Secretary of State."

"I appreciate the seminar on history and gossip, but is that really enough to jerk me out here with no formal presentation of a real problem?" I asked.

"There's a problem here," he said quietly. "Nearly four months ago, when it appeared that the FLQ, the separatist underground in Quebec, was about to surface, I sent a young agent into Vancouver to observe things. To try and isolate the people and groups peddling the agency infiltration rumors.

"Williamson was the agent's name, and he reported faithfully, usually with news that had just been printed in Vancouver's *Province* or *Sun,* or one of the Victoria papers. Somebody turned *him* in as the propagandist, to the RCMP, and they investigated. Sure enough; there was one of our agency men in place, in Vancouver.

"Did damned little good to notify B.C. mountie headquarters that Williamson's presence had been approved by Ottawa. The incident irritated our State Department because it was only another abrasive particle involved in a rising tide of Canadian protest against our overwhelming ownership of their business and industry.

" 'The Committee for An Independent Canada' was formed, to safeguard Canada's independence from the United States, and its membership grew rapidly. Not wild-eyed zealots, either; many big political, business, and industrial names joined it. A new, more favorable contract was signed by Ottawa with the People's Republic of China, to deliver in three years 6.9 million long tons of Canadian wheat.

"Then, two months ago, events in Canada exploded with a vengeance. First, the Ottawa Government officially recognized mainland China, and closed all the Taipeh diplomatic offices in the country. British diplomat James Cross and Quebec Labor Minister Pierre Laporte were kidnapped, and Laporte assassinated. Prime Minister Trudeau stopped being a peripatetic mod swinger and invoked the total security War Measures Act, which gave him absolute control. Three hundred and sixty-two arrests were made in Quebec in three days, all without warrants, and every major government figure and his family were furnished with armed guards.

"Williamson, our plant in Vancouver, had been sending his garbage reports in serenely, until three weeks ago. When they stopped, we asked the B.C. mountie headquarters to check on him, since Ottawa obviously had its plate full. Vancouver RCMP could find nothing. But, they reported, Vancouver Alderman J. Donald Atwater, a longtime showboat local pol and proponent of union with the United States, had requested a security guard.

"His life, he said, had been repeatedly threatened. He was advised that if he delivered his next publicized pro-Yank speech, scheduled for a meeting of the Vancouver Council tomorrow, he would be killed. . . ."

Pearsall reached inside his expensive hacking jacket and handed me a long red wallet with Air Canada's insignia imprinted on it in white. It was bulky.

"Here, U.S. currency, Canadian, a passport in the name of Richard Gardner, a receipt and key for a Robson Street apartment in Vancouver. No need to register; just go up the elevator. Another receipt and key for a Victoria apartment, same thing. The usual paper impedimenta in the Gardner name: international vaccination certificate, U.S. driver's license, etc.

"You will take the B.C. ferry from Swartz Bay, in . . ." Pearsall glanced at his watch, ". . . about forty minutes. Puts you in Vancouver at 8:40. Get a bus, not a cab, to the apartment, then call Miss Kelly Wu at this number. She is Atwater's private secretary. He owns a string of hardware stores, and real estate in Vancouver, Victoria, Prince George, and Prince Rupert. Miss Wu is privy to all his business and aldermanic affairs. You are supposedly a consultant he has called in from the States, to advise him on an expansion program."

"In the hardware business?"

"Right." Pearsall took out a flax handkerchief and mopped at the corners of his mouth, then all over his dew-lapped bulldog face. "Find Williamson, if you can. Has, or had, a wife and two young kids. I'm flying out in half an hour. If you need anything, I'll get it to you as soon as I can. Okay?"

"Yes, sir," I said. He walked away, limping slightly, down the darkened aisle, past the displays of wax dummies. The tails of his jacket swung loosely, and the furled umbrella was hooked over his right arm. He did not glance at any of the dummies, since his life was spent in dealing with live and dangerous ones.

I gave him ten minutes, went back to have another look at Bach, and walked out of the museum. The girl with fat thighs was chewing gum behind the cash register, and I nodded as I pushed out into the early, overcast darkness.

The bus station was across the street. I boarded the ferry bus to Swartz Bay, and in less than four hours was going up in the automatic elevator, in the Robson Street high-rise apartment. Mine was on the tenth floor, and had the neutral sterility of luxury apartments everywhere. Fully furnished, linen, china, crystal, and everything necessary for the full life. Wide sliding windows looking out over the Georgian Towers, the Bay Shore Inn, and Vancouver harbor.

A small brochure by the telephone proudly announced that the apartment had pastel-colored kitchen and bath appointments, and double-plumbing. I could not understand what for, but had another look. Everything in the kitchen and bath was pale blue, but I could not detect the double-plumbing. Overload? One useful in event the other failed? I had not thought Vancouver got that cold. So it was just another addition to the millions of things I did not understand.

I called the telephone number of Miss Kelly Wu, and, when it answered, cringed from the strident pound of blaring acid-rock music. A feminine voice answered, saying Miss Wu here, and I asked why she was trying to ruin her ears.

"Not really," she answered. "What's your problem?"

"You, at the moment. I just arrived from the States. My name is Gardner, and I understand that Mr. Atwater is going to make a speech tomorrow to the Vancouver City Council."

"That's right. At four o'clock. And you would be the cat from—"

"Not on the phone, Miss Wu," I interrupted. "Would it be all right if I came by your office at three tomorrow afternoon?"

"No. Mr. Atwater said no. You're supposed to meet me at 4:30 P.M. in the Mozart Konditorie, on Robson. We'll wait there."

"Okay." The music was still blasting at my eardrums. "Don't you know, Miss Wu, that Janis Joplin was found dead with a spike in her arms, and that Jimi Hendrix went for a big yellow-bird ride and choked to death on his own vomit?"

"Yes," she answered promptly. "I read all about it. Now if you'll just take off your high-button shoes and hindering truss, I'm sure you'll have a good night."

The phone clicked, and she was off the line. Smiling, I went to the shower, and in my pajamas fought the strange bed for a comfortable position. . . .

CHAPTER EIGHT

KELLY AND I decided we didn't want a pizza after all. Or at least the tall Chinese girl decided it for us. We walked on down the midnight steets of central Vancouver to Hastings on the water front, and stopped by the Canadian Pacific wharf to watch a white merchant vessel being loaded. The ship's lines were clean, and her superstructure one-stack and modern. She looked to be about ten thousand tons. All five of her hatches were open and lighted winches were swinging containerized cargo into them.

The illuminated merchant ship was bow-to from where we stood, so I could not make out her name or identify her house flag. Kelly Wu said she was the *Dong Feng,* which meant east wind. She had been built for the People's Republic of China in West Germany a few years ago, and worked out of Canton. When I asked Kelly how most of the Chinese community in Vancouver stood on the subject of the two Chinas, she said that opinions did not split on the matter of age groups. Many older Chinese had been hurt by Chancre Jack's headlong flight from mainland China, and not many in any age group considered his overaged army on Formosa a threat to anything except the U.S. Treasury.

We walked on south to Water Street, and found Gastown alive and flourishing. This rehabilitated slum section, once the main waterfront area of Vancouver, represented the other side of the coin from the indolent hippie panhandlers we had seen on Robson Strasse. Here, as in so many depressed areas I had seen while working on various contracts, the underground people were attempting to create a counterpart society. One to rival the hated Establishment.

Here in Gastown they had done it with considerable flair and expertise. The boutiques, cafes, coffeehouses, and saloons were visually interesting, hand-decorated, and mostly the wild graphics came off. The young dropouts and protesters, in this area, were largely Yank deserters and draft-dodgers in a strange land which had offered them asylum. They had transformed condemned flophouses into Wizard-of-Oddish hotels with farout wall murals, and many of them were attending the University of British Columbia or Simon Fraser University while developing their unusual business establishments.

Kelly and I went into a coffeehouse for a cup of espresso, and in the packed, colorful gloom found ourselves surrounded by a horde of bearded young men and headbanded women. Babies were there too, even at that hour, but they all seemed fat and healthy. The difference was one of tempo; the languid drifters downtown had seemed an unwarranted plague. Here, in the smoky coffee shop, we seemed to be in a den of busy kulaks, concentrated and plotting against the existing order.

We went strolling on, turning west, then south again, and came to an even livelier enclave. Not just a few blocks, either. The streets were brightly lighted, and noisy. Neon dragons belched scarlet flames, and speakers outside record shops blared monotonous music. The sidewalks were crowded with shoppers inspecting the contents of grocery-cum-flower shops, meat markets featuring glazed ducks and chickens, and narrow stores offering lichi nuts, ginseng, and other oddments.

This busy inner city was the Vancouver Chinatown, second largest on the Pacific Coast. As we got into the second block, Kelly Wu's swinging passage, in her dark pantsuit and matador hat, turned into a triumphal welcome. Bent old Chinese men bowed to her, lounging Chinese teenagers with ragged locks shouted "Hi, Kelly!," and the tall girl swept onward laughing and answering their greetings.

"My God," I murmured. "It's all clear now. You have brought me down here amongst all these inscrutables to Shanghai me, force me into a life of shame and degradation."

"Mr. G.," she answered crisply, "you've guessed it. However, those varicose veins are going to knock the price down sharply."

She turned into a doorway I would not even have noticed, and went up a littered stairway. Which, at the top, turned into a huge room with a dance floor in the center, a bar beyond, and cavernous fringes filled with tables. "K&W Gardens" winked the small neon sign over the bar.

Most of the tables were empty, but Kelly Wu's entry brought smiling greetings from the lounging waiters and busboys. She nodded to them, and swung on toward a large table beside the bar. It was round, and could have seated a dozen people. When I remarked on this, Kelly said "oh, hush" and sat down. A waiter shuffled forward with two flamboyant, scarlet menus, but was waved aside by a Chinese woman of middle age who smiled at both of us. Her face was classically beautiful, without any makeup I could detect, and she wore a dark cheongsam dress.

"Well, stranger," she said to Kelly, "it's been too long. What would you like to eat?" Snapping her long fingers at the waiter, she ordered him to bring tea and he took off like a rocket.

Kelly Wu ordered our food in Chinese. Won ton soup, shrimp-fried rice, sweet-and-sour spareribs, and egg rolls. The hostess nodded, watched the waiter put the big teapot on the table, and repeated the order to him. While he was bowing and retreating, the serene hostess poured tea and remarked to Kelly, still in Chinese, that her escort seemed a trifle old.

Kelly shrugged. He is a Yank, she answered, a friend of Mr. Atwater's. Then, abruptly, she said in English, "Mr. Gardner, may I present my aunt, Mrs. Li?"

I was lighting one of the small Dutch cigars, and stood up. "Mrs. Li," I said, bowing.

The hostess with the scrubbed and fine-boned face

shook hands. Her grip was cool, brief, and firm. "It is a pleasure to have you here, sir, especially in such radiant company."

"Madame, I was abducted from a pizza parlor, without warning."

She smiled and turned back toward the cash register. Kelly and I sipped at the scalding tea. The huge restaurant was pleasantly ramshackle, making only a halfhearted effort to introduce Chinese symbols, and it looked well worn and used. Several young men were standing at the bar, about twenty feet away from us. Three of them were hippies, two young Chinese in business suits, and their interest seemed to be focused on the gesturing young man at the far end of the bar.

He was not tall, but lithe, almost leonine, and wearing tight mod clothes, all black, and knee-high black boots. A mix, not pure Chinese, and I thought possibly a cross with West Coast Indian. That made his moon face seem a clash of two cultures. His hair was jet black, long, but not moppish. It was molded smoothly into a dark casque over his ears. He was haranguing his bar comrades, and they were all laughing on cue.

"Why the big hello?" I asked Kelly. "Are you the illegitimate great granddaughter of Sun Yat-Sen?"

She laughed, sipping at her tea. "Here?"

"No, ever since we entered Chinatown."

"Oh . . . I grew up here. My father owns this restaurant."

The old waiter shuffled back to the table, his face set, and put two drinks down on the table.

"Who, Charlie?" asked Kelly Wu. He turned his head toward the bar. She told him to take the drinks back, but not to charge him for them.

"Charge who?" I asked quietly. "The *métis* loudmouth? The cat with the beauty-parlor hair?"

"That's right. His name is Chong Chan, and I went to high school with him. Sort of a hard boy, but strictly minor league. Has held up a few grocery and candy stores, served short prison terms. Several years ago I went out with him, against my parents' advice. A few times was enough but he still calls me."

I had another look at the mixed-blood Hamlet in the tight black clothes. . . . And met his baleful stare. Conversation at the bar had fallen off to nothing.

"He's upset about your refusing the drinks," I told Kelly quietly, "and may try me. I hope not."

"They're watching him," she answered, but her gaiety was gone. The Won ton soup arrived, and we both attacked it with porcelain paddles. I was nearly halfway through mine when I saw Chong Chan approaching the table, carrying a depleted drink in his right hand.

"I am sorry you were offended," he said, stopping between us. Speaking to Kelly, but looking at me. He sounded sober, but I was watching his hand tighten around the glass.

"Oh, Tommy, why must you be such an ass!" Kelly said irritably, and he threw the drink in my face. Watered Scotch. Some of the ice cubes bounced down into my soup. The boys at the bar were watching.

"My friend," I said in Mandarin, "I have not harmed you, and do not wish to. You are being unwise."

Kelly stared at me in astonishment, and Tommy Chan frowned uncertainly. He backed away holding the empty glass, set it on the bar and went walking swiftly across the restaurant and down the stairs. I got up, pawing more ice cubes out of my napkin, and walked past the bar toward the men's room. There I mopped myself off, urinated, and combed my hair. As I was finishing this process, a toilet flushed and a tall, immaculately clad Chinese came out of the stall and joined me at the wash basins.

He was thin, well over six feet tall, and the suit he was wearing hung on him with Savile Row correctness. A sword-blade face, with carefully styled dark hair. He glanced at me, once, washed and dried his hands, and walked out. I followed him, and found the rest of the food on the round table. While we were tucking into it, I asked Kelly if she knew a Chinese of middle age, very urbane, who wore London-cut suits.

She nodded, gnawing at a fragrant sparerib. "My Uncle Li. An importer, has shops here, in Victoria, Montreal, and Toronto. Quite the toff. That was his wife you met earlier."

"Where is your father, the proprietor?" I asked, and she laughed.

"Here from four in the afternoon until nine at night. Never later. He supervises the kitchens closely, but really hates the joint. My mother hasn't been in it, except for festival days, since I was a little girl."

"Why did Tommy Chan take off? He was all wound up to take a punch at me."

Kelly had another portion of almond chicken. "You threw him off balance," she chortled. "Speaking Chinese, I mean. He doesn't know a word of it. Where did you learn it?"

"Flying into Kunming and Chungking," I said. "Across the Himalayas."

We finished the dinner, or at least presently had enough, since no one ever finishes a dinner in a real Chinese restaurant. I called for a check, but the serene lady with the scrubbed face materialized and said that the Gardens were privileged to have such visitors. There was no check. I tucked a five-dollar bill under a plate, nodded, and thanked her.

Our passage out of the cavernous restaurant was the same as our entrance. Everybody loved Kelly Wu, the Chinese matador. It was now nearly two o'clock in the morning, and we caught a cab back to my apartment building, had too many cognacs, and made love. It had been a long day.

CHAPTER NINE

I AWAKENED at six in the morning because someone was punching me in the back. Blearily, I removed the pillow from my head and tried to remember where I was. *Ah, there, Vancouver, British Columbia. . . .* The party tormenting me was a naked young Chinese girl with small but perfectly formed breasts. I put my head between them and inquired why she was abusing me so.

"You snore like a *gaijan* fiend," she said.

"Ah, well," I answered, withdrawing from this warm sanctuary. Like MacArthur, I stated that I would return. As for the snoring, God puts burdens on all of us. What time did the morning Vancouver *Province* come out? Fleeing toward the bathroom naked, Kelly murmured something about seven o'clock.

I picked up the telephone, dialed the desk downstairs, and asked if we could get breakfast. Indeed, we could. I ordered a pot of coffee for four, two double orange juices, two mushroom omelettes with a side order of Canadian bacon, crisp, and whole wheat toast. The polite fellow at the other end said they had some nice mangoes. I said certainly, with a quartered lime. Was the morning paper in yet?

"Just came, sir. We'll send one up with the breakfast."

"Thanks," I said, and hung up to see Kelly emerging from her shower, still naked, toweling vigorously at her dark hair.

"Miss Kelly," I said, "if you'd just step over here, I'd like to have a word with you." She did, and the rest of it was wordless. There is little in the literature about the advantages of hangover love. Much can be said for it. You exist in a confining haze, with a throbbing head, but the perception is direct. And the satisfaction extreme.

When the door chimes sounded half an hour later, I leaped out of bed to open it. The smiling waiter pushed his car inside, and from the aluminum compartments under it began to set out the hot plates. I opened the folded copy of the Vancouver *Province* and found that I had made the frong page.

The headline read "*ALDERMAN ATWATER ATTACKED TWICE, KILLED.*" The subhead announced that "*U.S. ASSOCIATE FOILS INTRUDERS.*" That seemed silly, since he had been kicked to death before our eyes, so how could I have "foiled" the intruders? I was referred to as Mr. Richard Gardner, consultant and business advisor to the late Mr. Atwater.

Kelly Wu was drowsing, so I shook her awake, complaining that she snored dreadfully. She stuck out her tongue at me, and put on my dressing gown. We sat down to the sumptuous breakfast. After I had poured us both coffee, I read her the lead story in the *Province*.

The tall Chinese girl was slicing her mango when I told her that I would have to move. Right away, because of the newspaper publicity. And that I would also have to change names and passports.

"Just like that?" she asked.

"Just like that."

"Then you are an American agent?"

I had a bit more of the omelette.

"Okay. Mr. Atwater, the late Mr. Atwater that is, had many real estate holdings in Vancouver. A good many of the apartments are furnished. Do you want one of them?"

"If you realize that because I belted out those intruders, my life will be in danger as long as I remain in British Columbia, yes."

Kelly Wu nodded. She was a portrait of a desirable woman as my dressing gown, parted, hung loosely on her while we finished our breakfast. In an hour, we were gone from the expensive high-rise apartment, leaving only the littered mobile table from which we had eaten.

CHAPTER TEN

IN AN HOUR, Kelly and I looked at a couple of apartments, and I selected one and moved in while she went down to the office. As I was unpacking my case twenty minutes later, a knock came at the door. A chunky fellow in coveralls said he was the custodian of the apartment building, and that Miss Wu wanted to talk to me on the phone.

I followed him down to the lobby pay phone, and the Chinese girl told me that Assistant RCMP Commissioner Henning wanted to see me. Did I want the apartment phone turned on?

"Yes, please," I said, and after hanging up I tried to tip the watching custodian. He refused it, saying that his salary was adequate. But that if he got in a bind, he might try to borrow some money from me. He wasn't arrogant about it, just factual. I shook my head and went back to get my raincoat.

At mountie headquarters I was shown directly to Henning's office, and the tall, balding man gave me the perfunctory handshake again.

"We've found your chap Williamson," he said, "and the news is distressing. He's dead, killed in rather a messy way. In an empty trapper's cabin, in the wilderness outside Prince Rupert. And we didn't really find him; an anonymous caller tipped us to his location. Won't you sit down?"

"Thanks." I sat in the stiff chair before his wide desk. On the wall behind the desk were the crossed standards of Canada and the Union Jack, with a gold-framed portrait of Queen Elizabeth between them.

"We don't know why he was in that area, or how long he had been there. Prince Rupert's not a large place, y'know. His name does not show up on any hotel or motel registry there for the last two months. He was systematically tortured, both physically and psychologically, and the exact cause of death won't be known until after autopsy, for which we'll need your approval."

Williamson was the young agent who had preceded me into British Columbia, and vanished.

"I'm authorized to give that," I said. "No suspects?"

"None at present. The cabin was empty because its owner died last spring. We have four men working on the case. Would you like to go up and have a look round?"

"No, sir. Your people are far better equipped than I am, for that."

Henning stroked his graying moustache with a forefinger, and nodded. I thought that in time he might even forgive me for having pulled him out of his home the night before.

Not that I was putting him on. In all of Canada's ten provinces except Quebec and Ontario, the RCMP are not only the provincial police but their authority extends to the smaller cities and towns as well. Metropolitan areas like Vancouver and Victoria have their own forces, but the mountie writ runs everywhere else.

"The body and evidence were flown down this morning in one of our planes," said Henning. "One thing in particular will interest you, I think."

"Oh?"

"Yes. Hanging from Williamson's right earlobe was another of the white wolverine figurines. It is also hand carved, and appears to be an exact replica of the one found piercing Atwater's ear."

He pushed back his chair and got up, suggesting that we go have a look at what had been flown down from Prince Rupert. I followed him down to the evidence room, and said good morning to Harry, my Irish compatriot. He got the Williamson file box. A tweed topcoat which smelled terrible, a water-soaked wallet and attaché folder, and a

Colt Police Special .38 in a snap-on hipholster. The weapon had not been fired.

Finally, another of the snarling wolverine talismans, its chain and barb darkened by dried blood.

"No baggage, personal effects?" I asked. Our agents usually carried several thousands of dollars in currencies differing according to the assignment area, but the wallet and attaché folder were empty.

"Nothing," said Henning. "His pockets had been rifled, also." He reached for the sheaf of papers hanging inside the file box, riffled through them, and showed me one signed by the RCMP Medical Officer in Prince Rupert. The report stated that the deceased had been heavily medicated for ten days or a fortnight prior to his death with a drug called succinylcholine.

This drug, the report continued, was a quick-acting muscle relaxant which paralyzed the body while allowing the patient to remain fully conscious. Under its influence, the patient's respiratory action often stops for as long as two minutes, and he experiences "a vivid fear of imminent death." The medication had been used briefly in California State Hospitals, in treating intractable patients, but was now forbidden there except in cases where the patient's written consent was granted. To his knowledge, added the RCMP Medical Officer, no such consent had been given for at least two years.

I took a deep breath.

"Horror story, sir, innit?" asked Harry, and I nodded. It was just that, a horror story. Assistant Commissioner Henning said the bottles which contained the succinylcholine were in the morgue with the body of Williamson.

We walked back to his office, and I asked if I could have a list of the museum native-art curators in the Vancouver area, including both the University of British Columbia and Simon Fraser University, and of the shops which sold such authenticated objects. Henning nodded, and said it would be ready in a few minutes. I sat in the main hall waiting, my hands between my knees.

Prince Rupert is almost up to Alaska, on the Pacific

shore. It has heavy rainfall, and, except in the winter months, has a growth rate which is almost tropical. Fern forests, dense underbrush . . . I was thinking of Williamson trapped in the remote cabin back in that rank growth, lying motionless with his eyes staring, waiting for his breathing to start again.

This revery was interrupted by a pretty secretary who handed me two typed sheets. I thanked her and left the RCMP headquarters, buttoning my coat against a cold rain. At the corner cab rank I made a deal by the hour with the driver, and started down the list of people who might know something about the small wolverines carved in walrus ivory.

CHAPTER ELEVEN

THE FIRST four names listed were all in shops in downtown Vancouver, and turned up blank. They had never handled such wolverine figures; indeed they could not remember many wolverines carved in any material. Walrus, seal, moose, caribou, fox, and polar bear they had in plenty, many of them carved by Eskimo artists in soapstone, with attached parchments from the Canadian Government proclaiming them authentic. The price tags were authentic, too. In one cathedral-hushed place I touched a black totem pole less than two feet high and found it cost $954.

The inevitable conclusions were that the wolverine was not a favored subject, and that the ones connected with the two murders were not in commercial supply. That led me to direct the driver to the University of British Columbia, with its beautifully designed buildings set in gardened open spaces.

In the Fine Arts Department there, I caught Professor Harold Slocumb just leaving his office for a class. He unlocked his office door again, said he would meet the class and give the cretins in it something to occupy their tiny minds for awhile. Then he could give me ten minutes, no more. Slocumb was a brisk, elderly man with thick glasses almost obscured by his hair. I thanked him, and sat waiting in his small office while he loped away.

When he came back, I outlined the purpose of my quest. He was perched on the edge of his crowded desk, and nodded impatiently at my spiel.

"Yes, I know the man. Not an Indian or Eskimo, however, far from it. Does only wolverines; they're vicious bastards, you know. He has done some large ones in stone, and the smaller ones, such as you describe, in walrus ivory. Enormous vitality! Now let's see. . . ."

The mop-haired professor bounced around his desk and began to burrow in one of the stuffed drawers, muttering that he simply *must* create some order out of this chaos soon, came up clutching a paper, and told me peevishly to write the facts down, man; I was holding him up.

"Okay," I said. "Fire at will."

"His name is Gorde Ferguson. Lives in a lodge near nothing on the Skeena River. A full disability war-wounds soldier in the Second-To-End-All. Before that was a cattleman up in the Cariboo. The nature of his wounds, I know not. Scottish, fifty-three years old. Operates a wholesale meat-catering service to camps and resorts in the area. Highly unsociable, I'm told.

"His daughter, Mrs. Mavis MacPherson, markets his work when and if he chooses to turn it out. Several museums have offered to commission sculptures by him, of his own subject choice, but he has always turned them down. The daughter attended several of my classes, and now lives in Victoria, on the island. Her address there is 23 Mayfair Lane."

Thrusting his source paper back into the overflowing drawer, Professor Slocumb started shooing me out of his little office. "I have about forty minutes," he said, "to try to pump some knowledge of the wonder of the world into a sea of blank-faced ruminants. Nice to meet you, and even better to leave you."

The professor went loping away again, toward his waiting cretins, and I walked back to the cab smiling, knowing that there was at least one chance for a breakthrough at the University of British Columbia. Rain was still falling, and I told the cabbie to take me to the newly occupied apartment.

I had been inside it only a few minutes when the door buzzer sounded. I opened it, and a plainclothes RCMP man flashed his credentials and had me sign for a message. I didn't try to tip him. When the door was closed, I ripped the sealed envelope open and found a fax copy of an RCMP message from Prince Rupert to Vancouver, on the Williamson case.

The message, marked urgent to Henning, said that a torn piece of kraft paper, similar to the type used in stores, had been found wedged between logs, under the bunk on which Williamson had died. The shaky message scrawled on it said:

10 DOWNING STREET . . . 10 DOWNIN

That was a stopper. Had Williamson been hallucinating under the terror drug? Why, if he had been momentarily sane, had he been zeroed in on the British Prime Minister's official residence, thousands of miles away? The message ended by saying that a copy was being forwarded to Washington, D. C., for comparison with Williamson's handwriting.

As the girl in the rabbit hole said, *curiouser and curiouser. . . .* I went to the telephone, lifted the receiver, and got a dial tone. That Kelly Wu was worth her weight in imperial jade. After placing a person-to-person call to Mrs. Mavis MacPherson, 23 Mayfair Lane in Victoria, I lighted a small Willem two cigar and waited. No, I did not know the number.

The operator found it for me, and the phone burred. It was answered after five rings by a low voice I could barely hear. The voice was a woman's, hesitant, and she said that Mrs. MacPherson was not at home.

I told the operator I would talk to this party, and did so, explaining that I needed to find Mrs. MacPherson soon. There was a long silence on the line. I repeated my request, and the hesitant voice said Mrs. Mac was in Vancouver, at the Hotel Georgia, but would be coming back on the ferry that afternoon.

"Thanks," I said, and rang off. I called the Hotel Georgia, and they had a Mrs. Mavis MacPherson registered—406. Would they ring her? They would, and did. An alto voice answered, and said it belonged to Mavis MacPherson. I explained the reason for my call, and Mrs. MacPherson admitted that her father was a sculptor, confined in subject to wolverines. She put them on the market when he turned them out, which was not often.

I asked if I could talk to her for twenty minutes, and got a cello laugh. "Not this day. In twenty minutes I'm leaving the hotel in a taxi, to take the ferry back to Vancouver

Island. And I'm fighting a three-year-old man who is more active than a hunting tiger. If you are in Victoria, look me up and I'll be glad to tell you about my father's sporadic production. . . ."

"Lady," I said, "my business can't wait. I'll see you on the ferry." And hung up. I needed a shower, but had no time to take one. Shoving some laundered underwear, socks, handkerchiefs, and toilet articles into the Air Canada bag, I zipped it up and called a cab.

CHAPTER TWELVE

THE BUS marked Victoria was loading as I jumped out of the cab. And, with five minutes to spare, bought a round-trip ticket on the Tsawwassen ferry. Then I found out I need not have worried. Although there was a long line waiting, new arrivals simply strode to the head of it and clogged things up by passing people who had been waiting half an hour. Most of these mob-creators were doughty old ladies in sensible British Walker shoes and embellished chamber pots for hats. If admonished, either by the waiting public or bus drivers, they responded with acid retorts on the grave fall of character in people now using the facilities.

There were also some little old men, but they were mostly shrunken appendages with reedy laughter pushed through ill-fitting false teeth. I found them everywhere in British Columbia, these ancient old Empire types; mostly they were English or Scottish. I also found, after tangling with a couple of them, that the doughty old ladies were getting stronger every day. The little old men, on the other hand, were dropping like flies.

In self-protection, the bus company simply loaded its lead vehicle full, dispatched another, loaded it, and so forth. This way they did not even have to talk to the old ladies. I got in the second bus out; as we left, a third was filling rapidly. I had not seen a young woman with a small boy anywhere. The bus ran south through the Vancouver suburbs and twenty miles more to the ferry slip. On the way, we passed through a short tunnel under the Fraser River.

Sitting in the darkness under the river, I tried to get the

geography straight in my head. Vancouver, British Columbia, was a glittering seaport city of nearly half a million people, only a few miles north of the U.S. border on the Pacific. From it, two ferries operated to Vancouver Island, which was nearly three hundred miles long, surrounded by the Pacific, the Strait of Juan de Fuca, and the Georgia Strait.

The Canadian-Pacific ferry runs directly from Vancouver Harbor to Nanaimo, on the island. The other, operated by bus to Tsawwassen on the mainland and by ship from there, goes to Swartz Bay on the island, and fifteen miles more on the bus into Victoria, southernmost and largest of the island cities. This service, the one I was on, was operated by the Province of British Columbia.

It was still raining when the bus rolled on board the *Queen of Vancouver* ahead of the automobile traffic. We all trooped through the big ferry's bowels to the stairway, and upstairs. I walked around the two decks as the ship filled up, but could not detect anyone who seemed to be Mrs Mavis MacPherson. The ferry was lightly loaded, since it was past the tourist season, but I saw several turbanned Indians, dark moon-faced families which I took to be Pacific Coast Indians, and a high sprinkling of Chinese and Japanese.

There could even have been an Eskimo there, for all I knew. I have never seen an Eskimo, to my knowledge, but understand they anticipated us in wife-swapping. Between such lesser tribes and the Soviet Union, we Yanks haven't really discovered anything. The restaurant was closed, but I looked over the jammed cafeteria twice. No luck there, either. I was making the breezy top deck again when I glanced automatically at a pair of good legs at the rail. The wind whipping the short skirt proved that no artifice had been employed. The slender body on top of the legs turned and became a girl–woman with a ragged mop of tawny hair. Peeping out from the top of her zipped parka was another head, smaller, blonder, and crowing.

"Mrs. MacPherson?" I inquired.

She nodded, impish glee in her green eyes. The cold wind had put color on her cheekbones. "You've passed us twice," she announced over the wind. "So obviously looking for a small child that I smuggled Malcolm out of sight."

"Seems a nice little tyke," I roared, and Malcolm spat at me. Since he was in a privileged sanctuary. I could not respond in kind. "How about going inside?" I shouted. She nodded, pointed at a monstrous rope-handled carry-all, and I followed her forward. The bulging canvas bag weighed about fifty pounds.

When we were settled in scuffed leather chairs behind the glass wall, Mavis MacPherson went swinging off with Malcolm the Tiger to the can. When she came back, I tried to ask her some questions but she would have none of them, saying that we would be on the damned scow for an hour and forty minutes. While she fed Malcolm, I was to watch Mount Roberts' snowy peak, and think good thoughts.

The rain had stopped, fitful sunshine was lancing through the overcast, and Mount Roberts' snowy peak was effective in an imitation Fuji way. Malcom ate well and promptly lost most of it on the frayed carpet. I went to the men's can, got some damp and dry paper towels, and transferred his offering to the nearest waste receptacle.

While I was doing this, the plump, little, blond boy sat playing with a set of keys she had given him. As I was sitting back down beside his mother, he hit me in the face with the keys. Just below the left eye. I returned the keys and stanched the slight bleeding with my handkerchief.

"Malcolm doesn't like you," announced his young mother.

I nodded, "That's allowed. Because I am beginning to dislike him, too."

Mavis laughed. Honestly, so that the full breasts quivered under her thin blouse. Putting Malcolm down, she told him to go annoy some strangers, and he went staggering off toward the turbanned Indian.

That slender gentleman had been reading a magazine, but when the little boy put a hand on his knee, he smiled and lifted him with one arm. Malcolm began talking a blue streak, pointing at his mother, the ocean, and the whole world. The *babu* smiled serenely, rocking him to the motion of the boat.

"The little jerk never said one word to me," I complained, and Mavis smiled and tucked the long legs under her short skirt.

"He's selective, Now what was it you wanted?"

I told her the lie about being affiliated with the new native-arts museum in Aspen, Colorado; how we were collecting a sculpture show of North American animals. Someone had mentioned her father's work to me, in Vancouver. . . . Oh, yes; Professor Harold Slocumb, at the University of British Columbia, He had spoken highly of her father's work, and of her own work as a student.

Mavis MacPherson eyed me for some time. I can usually tell when people know I'm lying; I've had a lot of practice at it. With her, I couldn't tell. Turning her gaze from me to her young son, still chortling in the *babu*'s lap, she answered.

Her father was not an artist in the ordinary sense, she said slowly. Until 1938, he had been a working, prospering cattleman in British Columbia's high Cariboo country. She had been born there, just before he joined the Seaforth Highlanders, in Vancouver. As a Sandhurst graduate who had resigned his commission, he was posted major in the Canadian Regiment. During the Italian campaign, in the Liri Valley, he had been wounded severely but had led his men out of a panzer ambush.

For this, she said, he had received the V.C. but had been hospitalized and—

"Wait!" I interrupted. "Your father got the Victoria Cross?"

She nodded, and I commented that there was no crap or political compulsion connected with the medal. *That no matter what street Gorde Ferguson walked down, in whatever town, all men there present should uncover. . . .* I was staring at the snowy crest of Mount Roberts.

Mavis MacPherson was watching me curiously. I shrugged; would she please tell me about her father's work?

Yes. Her mother had been unable to find help enough to work the caribou ranch while her father was recuperating in an English hospital, so they had sold off first the breeding stock and then the land itself. Going to Victoria, they had bought a small farm outside the city. Her mother had died two weeks before her father returned. She had acted as his housekeeper for a year, but his eyesight had been limited and he had increasingly resented being helped.

One morning she had awakened to find him gone with all his belongings. He had left her most of the money and gone up to a small settlement named Tintagel in the wild country between Prince George and Prince Rupert, in central British Columbia. Months later a box had arrived with several ivory-carved figurines in them. They were all of wolverines. The short note with them said he was well, and that he did the figurines at night, as a diversion.

With regard to his insistence on the wolverine as a subject, Colonel Ferguson had said only that he regarded the fierce little animal as the sole self-sufficient and completely free animal left alive. He made no mention of selling the figurines, but kept sending them to his daughter at irregular intervals. She did market them, and sent him the money.

"Could he have sold others, up there?" I asked.

Mavis MacPherson looked up. The turbanned Indian was standing there, holding Malcolm the Tiger, now fast asleep.

"Madame," he said softly, "this young man has told me many things I should know. Now, I think, he needs his mother."

As he transferred the sleeping child deftly, Mavis smiled her thanks, and the tall Indian bowed himself away.

"Once," she said, over the child's head, "a shop in Victoria wanted a good many of the wolverine figures. I wrote him about it, and he sent me back a one-word telegram. *No*, it said. However, I've got an account book on his sales stuck away somewhere, who bought how many, and I'll dig it out for you."

"Fine." The ferry was hooting for Swartz Bay, its slip on Vancouver Island. When the announcement came over the speaker system that all bus passengers were to report back to the vehicles, I hoisted her unwieldy canvas bag and followed her toward the stairs.

CHAPTER THIRTEEN

WE FOUND seats together because several people had gotten off the bus at Swartz Bay. As it rolled off the ship, wheeling toward Victoria, Malcolm awakened in a bad temper. I was sitting in the aisle seat and Mavis had the big bag between her legs, on the floor. One after another, she tried to pacify him with toys from the bag, but he only howled and flung them aside.

A doughty old lady, sitting in the seat ahead of Mavis, turned to deliver a scathing comment about people who could not control their children, and Malcolm crushed her had with a dilapidated teddy bear. When she waxed indignant about this outrage, Malcolm nearly brained her with the remnants of a Tinker-Toy. That shut her up proper, and I began to change my opinion of the child.

Mavis was not embarrassed; she was too busy collecting things he had thrown away. Handing him to me without warning, she began to collect them. Malcolm tried to backhand me, and I zapped the little bastard firmly while his mother wasn't looking. But I was looking. Mavis had rolled so far forward, to grope under the seat ahead, that I had the definitive view of her pantyhose. They were not opaque.

"Lord?" I asked silently, looking upward while holding a protective forearm against the tot's onslaughts. "Have I to suffer this anguish, too?" And it suddenly occurred to me that not one word had been said concerning Mavis' husband.

When she rolled back level on her nylon-sheathed bottom, I gave the child to her and inquired about Mr. MacPherson's health.

"There is no Mr. MacPherson," she said angrily. "There was one, and you can just forget it!"

"Right." The bus was rolling through central Victoria, and I had a glandular imbalance. In the groin. We wheeled past Centennial Square, the restored City Hall, the inevitable Eaton's store, and swerved to rest in the small station behind the Empress Hotel car park.

When we were off the bus, and Mavis had collected another bag, this time a suitcase, I asked what now.

"For you, I don't know," she said. "But my plan is to catch a cab for three blocks, to the central bus stop at Douglas and Yates, and then catch another bus. It will take us to the end of the line, and then we will walk the odd mile to home."

I was horrified. Her clothes, while worn slapdash, had seemed to be of good quality. Now she was proposing several transfers of the obstreperous boy, the big handmade carryall, the suitcase, and a long walk at the end of it.

"That may do for you," I said, "but I want to see your father's sale register, and I don't propose to go through all those dodges. Let's get a cab, shall we?"

"It will cost you a lot of money," she warned, but I had already signaled to a cab. We loaded into it and went wheeling back the way we had come, along Douglas Street. I had a faint premonition when I saw that the cab meter was set on eighty cents before it started. Sometimes, not often, I wish I could separate my contract objectives from my gonads.

Malcolm was asleep again, nestling in his mother's left arm. The cab passed the Hudson's Bay Company Emporium, and rolled on. In about twenty minutes, over roads of which I had no knowledge, it stopped at a country place north of Victoria. The house was manor-style English, not large, but two storied and surrounded by trees. To the right, a large garden, with some evidence of failed topiary art on its neglected hedges. A large garden.

As the cab was stopping, Mavis looked at me over the head of her sleeping child and said calmly, "If you had any idea of helping us, and finding bed and breakfast here, please forget it."

The meter on the taxi now read $8.60. When Mavis

had gotten out, I followed her with the cumbersome carry-all and the suitcase, and told the driver that I would be there half an hour. No more, and would pay waiting time, because I had to make the next bus to the ferry. Then I turned to Mavis.

"Can he get a cup of coffee while you are showing me your father's sales register? Maybe a sandwich?

"Yes," she said. "We don't have a cook, only a kitchen slavey. But I'm sure she could manage a coffee and something to eat."

The cab driver was a gaunt, mixed-blood type. Sallow-faced. He said that would be fine, and I told him that I would send a drink to the kitchen, too, if any was going. Greasy hair spilling out from under his frayed cap, he agreed to this possibility. I followed Mavis toward the lighted doorway, across the cobblestoned walk.

She took sleeping Malcolm up the stairs, and I put the carryall and suitcase at the foot of them and drifted into the living room. It had the usual bibelots and pictures, the stand at Omduram, the Boer War, the Tattoo by bear-skinned warriors, with colors rippling. The leaded casement windows were open; it was much milder here than in Vancouver.

Mavis came back down the stairs in a hostess coat, glittering with Hong Kong silver threads. She went to a carved cabinet, unlocked it, and set a decanter before me. Walked down a hall to the right and came back with a huge, tarnished silver bowl full of ice cubes and three splits of soda. I asked for a small tumbler-type glass, and she brought me one.

After a straight shot of the Scotch whiskey, I requested that she take a drink back to the cab driver.

She filled a glass, and went back to the kitchen. I was pouring another drink when someone started shooting at me from the gathering darkness of her garden. I spat out the drink on the way to the floor, scrambling to get behind the couch.

CHAPTER FOURTEEN

THE ECHO of the shots racketed around the house as I lay prone, listening for some sound of movement in the darkened garden. When none came, I called Mavis and heard her low reply. She and the kitchen girl were on the floor; Malcolm was alone upstairs. I was unarmed because of the recently invoked War Measures Act. After the political kidnappings and murder in Montreal, all Canada was uptight about citizens carrying guns.

"Do you have a weapon in the house?"

"Yes. Dad's service revolver's back here. Loaded, but hasn't been fired since he left."

"Get it. Then crawl along the corridor until you can toss it to me. After that, go upstairs and keep Malcolm down, away from the windows."

"All right."

Soon she was hitching down the hallway on her elbows, and when I held my right hand out she threw me the leather-cased pistol. It was venerable but oiled, and I checked the load and switched the safety off. Scrambling across the hall to the darkened room on the side away from the garden, I opened one of the French doors and went stalking.

Waiting by a tall hedge, I let my eyes become accustomed to the darkness. Minutes went by with light glowing from the mullioned windows of the silent house. Far away, there were traffic noises, but they seemed remote from the garden's gloom. Finally a twig snapped near me and I lunged around the tall hedge. A handgun blasted twice, very close; I could see the muzzle flames.

Having no place to go but forward, I lunged at the place

they had appeared, triggering the pistol. It clicked but did not fire, and after I was clubbed down, the intruder bolted past me and into the kitchen door. And then I passed out, trying to follow him. . . .

When I recovered consciousness, I was lying half draped into the hedge, and blood from a scalp wound was dripping into my right eye. Wiping at it with my handkerchief, I eased back around the house and into the same French door by which I had left. The lights were still on in the living room, kitchen, and upstairs, but nobody was in the house, although the driver's greasy cap was on the kitchen floor.

His cab was gone. I looked for a telephone, but could not find it. Finally, in a hall alcove, I found the severed cord. In the bathroom, I examined my scalp laceration; it would not be fatal and I cleaned it as well as I could. Then, without even turning off any lights, I went walking down the quiet lane to the nearest house which showed any lights.

An elderly Englishman in a dressing gown answered my knock and listened to my story without visible emotion. Once or twice he harrumphed, as if in comment on the way the neighborhood was going downhill, then asked how he could help. When I said that I needed to get to RCMP headquarters, he nodded. In a few minutes we were tooling toward Victoria in an ancient but perfectly kept Bentley.

As we turned onto the main highway, Klaxons and sirens came rushing toward us. When they were nearly up to us, a speeding cavalcade of police and RCMP cars turned left down the Swartz Bay Road with the sounds of their passage keening through the night. Their lights were flashing, and traffic parted hastily. Acting on impulse, I asked my English benefactor to turn down that way.

When we were only a few miles from the marina and ferry slip, traffic began getting heavier and finally came to a halt. I asked the old gentleman to pull off on the shoulder and started out on foot. Not far ahead I came to a uniformed constable who had halted all vehicular traffic, and was trying ineffectually to stem the surge of pedestrians. I was one of them, and soon saw what was causing the jam up.

A battered car was on its side at the bottom of a twelve-foot ditch. One rear door was caved in; it had obviously rammed and ricocheted off another car, or something equally heavy. The windshield was shattered, with glass shards glittering like daggers. Up on the road an ambulance with its red light flashing was backed up to the ditch. Its attendants were struggling up the steep slope with a loaded stretcher.

The wrecked car was the taxi which had brought Mavis, her small son, and me out to the MacPherson house. The man carrying the front end of the stretcher stumbled, tried to regain his balance, and both the covering sheet and limp figure were dislodged. While the gawking spectators whispered, thrilled to pieces at this final indignity, I had a look at the corpse. It was the surly cab driver.

Not that being so unceremoniously tossed about made any difference now. Half his head had been shot away, from behind.

I moved back and away from the whispering spectators and found a police officer in his car. He had been reporting on radio to his station, and when he was through I explained my involvement with the corpse in the ditch, half of whose head was a bloody pulp. He asked a few questions, all intelligent, but it was clear that he did not believe me. Finally he reported what I had told him, with admirable brevity, to his station, and signed off. Then he told me that whatever had happened at the MacPherson house, the man who had killed the cab driver now commandeered a small private yacht. He was standing out in Swartz Bay in it, holding five hostages. When ordered to surrender, by hailer, from a circling RCMP launch, he had begun firing a rifle, wounding two police officers aboard.

A call came on his radio; he was ordered to bring me to the marina pier for small craft. We drove there, forcing a way through traffic with the Klaxon and light, and when we stopped I saw the small yacht half a mile offshore.

Pinned in a network of spotlights from launches circling just out of rifle range.

A more senior RCMP officer came to talk to me, and I explained again. Saying that three of the hostages had to be Mavis MacPherson, her son Malcolm, and the kitchen girl. He nodded, and added that the other two were the owners of the yacht, a Seattle insurance man and his wife, He didn't believe me, either. Oh, the possibility was in his mind, but he couldn't understand what the hell I had to do with the deal. And that was understandable, I suppose.

I asked what their plans were, and the mountie officer becoming a trifle shirty, said that they would simply keep the little yacht pinned down until its occupants ran out of food and water.

"Man," I said with exasperation, "you can't do that! There's a child aboard. Three women. And this cat has to be a psychopath. He has already tried to kill me from ambush, has killed the cab driver, so he can't get burned any worse in court. If you don't give him a little running room, some chance, he might just slaughter everybody on board."

The policeman was polite, but obdurate. In the States, we had our procedures; Canada had others. And it was plain that he thought the RCMP on the side of the angels in this connection.

"Unhunh," I answered. "Now, do me a favor, please. Get me a radio-telephone contact with Assistant Commissioner Henning. Tell him that the Yank who was in the Vancouver hospital when Alderman Atwater died wants this cordon of cruisers withdrawn from the captured Seattle yacht. That the Yank wants a wetsuit outfit immediately. No breathing apparatus, just wetsuit, facemask, and flippers.

"That he also wants the launch with the hailer to approach as nearly as possible to the seized yacht, and inform its captor that he is free to take the vessel into American waters, across the Strait of Juan de Fuca. That he will not be hindered in his passage if he will agree not to harm any of his hostages. That a U.S. Coast Guard launch from the Port Angeles, Washington, station will meet him and take off the hostages without attempting to capture him. After that, he's on his own for forty-eight hours."

The RCMP officer stared at me with ill-concealed distaste. "Who the hell do you think you are?" he asked.

I sighed. "Nobody important, friend. But if you don't put that message through, I promise that Ottawa will leave you with considerable egg on your face."

The face tightened, and he wheeled away. Came back in twenty minutes and had me repeat my demands into the mike of a portable tape recorder. When he had stomped off again, I walked over to the marina bar and had a beer. When I asked one of the lounging yachtsmen how cold the water was in Swartz Bay and out in the strait, he said about 39 degrees in the bay, probably two degrees colder in the strait. On the surface. . . .

I nodded glumly. *Just what I wanted for Christmas. . . .* A man couldn't live very long in such water.

It took nearly two hours to get the message relayed, answered, and the operation put under way. Finally the circling cordon of launches was withdrawn, the offer made over the bull-throated electronic hailer, and an agonizing wait ensued while the beleaguered pirate-murderer calculated his chances. The police boat veered back toward the pier, hull spanking against the black water, and tied up.

The terms had been accepted, with the added proviso that the U.S. Coast Guard craft deliver fifty gallons of gasoline, in tins, to the captured yacht. We all stood watching as the small craft put out, moving on its auxiliary power toward the Strait of Juan de Fuca.

When it was out of sight around the southern headland, I pulled on the wetsuit and adjusted the faceplate and snorkel. Carrying the flippers, I walked barefooted onto the police launch, which had been refueled. It idled away from the dock, and roared to full power with no cabin or running lights. Sitting below, I had a final small cigar, pulled the mask in place, and slipped on the fins.

When we had rounded the point and were closing in on the small Seattle yacht, I went to the launch's locker and got a short-handled, steel-tipped gaff. Then went up to the rail and stood with spray blowing in my face, watching the yacht come back toward us. There were no stars; an overcast had blotted out everything, and a fine sleety rain was falling. That helped.

It helped because if the nervous cat at the helm of the small yacht ahead ever suspected that he had been double-crossed, that we were pursuing him and meant to board, he might start some impromptu slaughtering.

When I thought we had closed enough, I touched the shoulder of the crewman waiting beside me. He moved forward through the pitch darkness to tell the helmsman. When he did, the cruiser slackened speed to idling. I checked everything again and vaulted feet first over the rail into the choppy plain of dark water.

The water was a shock, even through the wetsuit. Arms trailing, the short-handled gaff held in my right, rubbered fist, I went hitchkicking underwater toward the yacht. When I was a hundred yards or so from it, I surfaced to calculate the remaining distance. The rain was falling heavier, pocking the heaving water, and I submerged again.

When I came up, I was less than ten feet from the yacht, on the windward side of it. Inside the rubber casque on my head I could barely hear the auxiliary motor's screw turning; like most small sailing craft, its power plant was not large. A few strokes took me to the aft end, away from the wheel side, and I went eeling up its side.

When I had my flippered feet firmly on the coaming, I lifted the faceplate and waited. The rain was a torrent now, and I couldn't see or hear anything. Inching around the stern end of the yacht, I dropped to the rear deck, lunged down the stairwell, and smashed the curved side of the gaff hook down on the head of the figure hunched behind the wheel.

The figure toppled to the cabin floor, rolled once, and lay staring sightlessly up at me. Tommy Chang, the mod Chinese-Indian drink-tosser. . . . His jet, smoothly molded pompadour was disarranged; his rifle, which had been canted beside the wheel, had clattered to the cabin floor. A punk who had been given a kill contract on me had blown it; then in panic shot an innocent man in the back of the head and gotten himself into an impossible corner, with five hostages. Some gunman. . . . I was fairly sure he was dead, because the gaff had been wielded with severity, and I had felt his head give.

The hostages were staring at me from the bunks on both sides. They were all bound and gagged. I untied Malcolm first, and he took a swing at me. Figures. I hugged the little bastard anyway, then untied his mother, the kitchen slavey, and the Seattle owners of the yacht.

Everybody went gabble-gabble, which was normal, of course, but I roared for them to shut up. They were rebellious but not mutinous, having been deprived of their chance to fill me in on their hour or two with danger. I instructed the Seattle owner to get the yacht back on a course for Swartz Bay, using all his running lights, and to fire off a flare, in that order.

Then I tried to contact Swartz Bay by the yacht's radiotelephone, but could not raise them. The owner admitted sheepishly that it had not been working well lately, which I took to mean the damned thing had been out of order for some time, and gave up. Mavis was cooing over Malcolm, and seemed unable to find anything wrong with him, although I could have suggested several things. The kitchen slavey, after being freed from her bonds and gag, accepted a drink of water from me with a blank face.

As if to say, at the starvation wages I'm getting, what indignity is next? She had a point.

When the rest of them were chatting compulsively, I hoisted Tommy Chang onto one of the bunks. Frisked him briskly. In an inside pocket of his black suede jacket, I found another of the small white wolverines carved in ivory. With chain and barb attached.

Staring at it, balancing to the increased speed of the yacht as it rounded the headland toward Swartz Bay, I heard the sirens of approaching police launches. This particular wolverine, I was meditating without relish, was meant for my earlobe. . . .

CHAPTER FIFTEEN

WE WERE HUSTLED through the curious crowd gathered at the Swartz Bay marina, put into police cars, and driven back to Mavis' house, still standing silent with the lights on and the doors open. For nearly an hour, we were interrogated; this ordeal did not end until Mavis stalked upstairs with Malcolm. The police, withdrawing, left guards front and rear of the house. Which was just as well, because the lane was choked with the cars of curious motorists.

Sitting on the downstairs couch, I poured a tall drink of the old Scotch and listened to the sounds of Mavis upstairs, putting the boy to bed. The kitchen girl working in the back of the house. Once the girl came to the living room doorway, holding the dead cab driver's greasy cap, and I told her to leave it in the hall, the police might want it.

After my third Scotch, I went into the downstairs half-bathroom and urinated. This was not as easy as it sounds because I was not the most suitably dressed dude on Vancouver Island; I still wore the wetsuit, was barefooted, and had a sodden blanket draped around my shoulders. Someone had thrown it over me while we were stepping ashore at the marina.

My clothes, I remembered, were still in the police car of the nameless cat who had thought me such a liar. After I had eeled out of and back into the wetsuit, I walked out the back door to explain this situation to the guard on duty there. Could he call headquarters and help me retrieve my clothes?

He suggested that I use the telephone to contact the

Victoria police dispatcher, who would solve my problem in jig time. I sighed and explained that I had finished McGuffey's First Reader, but that Tommy Chang, the intruding murderer, had cut the phone cord and disposed of the instrument. Nodding, he said that if I would just keep his post for a moment, he would nip across to the nearest house and phone the request in.

So, standing barefoot in the wet grass, with the damp blanket not helping the clammy rubber suit any, I kept the vigil until he came strolling back. The police car must have been still at Swartz Bay, because in less than half an hour my clothes were returned. After I had changed into them, in the small downstairs bathroom, I came out to find Mavis waiting.

She was holding a fresh drink, and the tawny blond hair was down around her shoulders. She wore a brocaded Mandarin housecoat with a flaring collar and sweeping hemline, and after I had sipped at the drink moved in to put both hands behind my neck and kiss me with shocking directness. When her body pressed against mine, I could feel the heat of her, naked inside the loose coat.

"Very nice," I said. "What's it in aid of?"

"Oh . . . " She kissed me again, more slowly. "Thanks from me, from Malcolm. The house rules have changed, too. You are entitled to bed-and-breakfast in this house, anytime. No reservation required."

I smiled a trifle sadly over her shoulder, at the faded pictures of Poona and Aden on the walls. "Nice to get something from Malcolm which is not a poke in the eye. I could have accepted your offer when my affairs were in a lull. Now they're not. May I see your father's register of sales on the little ivory wolverines?"

Mavis' full mouth tightened; she closed the attractive gap where the collar of the robe had parted and turned into the small library-study off the larger room. There, from an ancient rolltop desk, she got a faded red ledger and flipped through it swiftly. And found what I wanted toward the back. "Seven 2" wolverines, Eddie Tahsis, Nanaimo."

The date was nearly three months old. I had her check

the record twice more, but it was the only sizeable sale of the little figurines. The others were singles or doubles, with one triple order.

"Do you remember Eddie Tahsis?"

"Not very well. He called the house, then came out. "A *métis,* I think. He didn't question the price, and it wasn't low. May have been pure Indian, but I don't think so."

I showed her the small white wolverine figure I had taken from Tommy Chang's inner pocket. "Was this one of that lot?"

Mavis examined it carefully. "That lot . . . How would I know? But my father did it. Not the barb and chain, of course. He would never junk up his work like that. Although I suppose anyone with the proper equipment could . . ."

I nodded, and after she had closed the ledger kissed her. She was not so cooperative as she had been; instead, she was trembling against me, but not toward me. I tried to gentle her like a fractious mare, my hands stroking her arched back. Saying that for men like me, who prowled alone most of the time, only a certain type of woman could ignite the blowtorch. That she did, for me. But that we were suddenly caught up in events, and that I hoped to enjoy her bed-and-breakfast if another natural chance ever came. . . .

The comely English girl trembling against me began to weep. "Thank you very much," she said bitterly. "I'll sit here in my little house and knit, until Mr. Wrong returns!"

Something attacked me in the back of the knees, and I half-turned to see Malcolm, in a pale blue sleepsuit, pummeling away at the back of my legs. I released his mother, turning and kneeling, and Malcolm hit me another fair shot on the Adam's apple. When I straightened and went walking out the front door, he was still swinging. With his mother, half-crying and half-laughing, holding him back.

In half an hour I was back at the Swartz Bay ferry slip, and in forty minutes the ferry was cleaving between the islands, toward Vancouver, on the mainland. It seemed incredible, as I watched the choppy black water slide by, that I had known Mavis and her ferocious young son only a few hours. The emotional electricity had been startling; I would have given a lot to stop my stupid pursuits long ago to share her bed. Oh well, nothing like saving people's lives to make them hate you. . . .

CHAPTER SIXTEEN

WHEN I was back in the Vancouver apartment, I checked with Bert Harrellson, the *Province* reporter, by phone. He was in the city room of the paper, and when I asked if he had ever heard of an Eddie Tahsis, he had me spell the name and left me holding for several minutes. Returning, he said no; he didn't know the name, and there was nothing in the *Province* morgue about him.

He had heard something interesting, however. Around the lower courts, the bail-bondsmen's offices, and from his underworld contacts. A source outside Vancouver was reported to be pouring large amounts of cash into the city's dissident elements. There was talk of hidden arsenals, homemade explosives, and an approaching show of strength with government which would dwarf any previous riots, sit-ins, or demonstrations.

The blowoff would come in Victoria, these rumors insisted. . . .

Harrellson added that these unsubstantiated reports might add up to a neat collision course with an event which was fact. Harvey Crandall, U.S. Secretary of State, would be the guest of Provincial Prime Minister Bennett in Victoria's Parliament, next Friday. Five days from tonight. The obvious inference was that an embarrassing international incident could be created at that time. Secretary Crandall was not on an official visit, only holidaying with his family at the Empress Hotel in Victoria, but still . . .

I thanked him, and rang off. Made a report call on this possibility to Neal Pearsall, on the agency's Washington recording bank, and caught a cab to St. Paul's Hospital.

The man whose shoulders I had broken, during the fatal attack on Alderman Atwater, was still too heavily sedated to talk to, and when I went down the hall to the supposedly guarded room of the other intruder I found it empty.

The ward nurse explained that the man had escaped, sometime during the night.

"Oh?" I asked politely. Not the finest plug in the world for the vaunted RCMP. "With guards at his door and window?"

"He's gone," she said angrily, and stalked away. I watched her skinny white-stockinged legs and flat-heeled shoes retreating, and decided that they would be ideal for stomping out disease. My next stop was RCMP headquarters, where the officer on duty let me see the file on the escaped prisoner.

His name, established through his fingerprints, was Jean Belliveau; he was a former logger and mine explosives expert with a long criminal record. A total of nine years prison time served. A *métis*. Heavy drinker, womanizer, and violent. I asked for all his mug shots, and any other pictures they had of him, and in half an hour they had furnished me with a sheaf of glossy prints.

I had these put on the wire to the RCMP office in Victoria, and called Mavis. She was sleepy because it was after midnight, but I said I wanted her to go down to the mountie headquarters and look at the pictures being transmitted. Then she was to call me at the Vancouver number.

It was 2 A.M. before she called back. Her low cello voice sounded tired, but was distinct. Yes, Jean Belliveau and Eddie Tahsis were the same man, she said. The pictures she had just viewed at headquarters were of the man who had bought the seven small wolverine figures. I thanked her, apologized for dragging her into Victoria at that hour, and hoped she and Malcolm would sleep well for the remainder of it.

"Oh," she said idly, "the night air is very invigorating. And the driver who came for me quite young and handsome. A smasher, really. But we appreciate your thought. If you don't awaken us again, we might sleep very well."

"You and the driver, or you and Malcolm?" I inquired.

That joke was so bad she did the only possible thing. Hung up on me. Oh, well, I had brought it on myself. The important, immediate thing was that the blind hog had found an acorn. Something matched. We had tied a man to the wolverine figures.

Two hours later I was lifted off a heliport beside Burrard Inlet by one of the mountie whirlybirds. Its rotors lifted us up and off the small asphalted area and went crabbing north over the glittering lights of Vancouver's West End, a tremendous, jeweled pattern even at this late hour. Over the Georgia Strait we thrashed north to Bella Coola, and there in dawning light set down on the high school playground. There was no airport in the small town, and I ducked away from the helicopter carrying only my Air Canada flight bag.

From there it was a five minute walk to dockside, through the sleeping town kept alive by a timber-processing plant. The place was only a cleft in wooded hills, and as I walked through it, frost sparkled on the street and storefronts. The helicopter went racketing over my head, nearly blowing me off my feet as it swerved over the harbor, on its way back to Vancouver.

The street, approaching the docks, narrowed. A hotel to my right, and it had to be a hotel. There were no roads in Bella Coola longer than a few miles, no connection through the Chilcotin wilderness which had brought the telegraph to this sparsely settled West Coast of British Columbia. No land route from the incredibly beautiful central part of the province, the birch and lake pastures of the high Cariboo.

There was, however, a sizeable ship alongside the principal dock. The *Northland Princ*e, bound for Prince Rupert and Alaskan ports. Carrying my light handbag, I went up her gangplank, and in the lounge at top found nobody. Bella Coola was asleep, the ship was asleep, and the landlocked little port was still chill cold. And would be until the sun got over the steep mountains to the east.

I found the stairway to the flying bridge and wheelhouse, and invaded that sacred sanctum. The officer on duty was startled, and protested "you're not allowed up here!"

"My sacred and frostbitten ass I'm not," I replied. "You get the chief steward up here, chop-chop, and I'll leave you to your task of navigating the vessel while she's not moving."

He was young, the duty officer, and his mouth fell ajar. "You're a passenger from Bella Coola!"

"Never in this world. I'm a passenger from Vancouver. An RCMP helicopter just flew me up from there to join ship, and I must say that you run your business like a hog farm."

"Where are you going, sir?"

"To Prince Rupert."

"Right." The young duty officer picked up a phone and called somebody. In a few minutes, the *Northland Prince*'s steward came scrambling up to the bridge deck, took my bag, and I followed him down to a small but comfortable cabin. He was Irish, the steward, and had awakened so hurriedly that his red jacket was still bunched up around the back of his neck.

"Can I do anything else for you, sir?" he asked sleepily.

"Yes. A plate of sandwiches and a bottle of rye whiskey."

"Oh, no, sir. Not possible." His sleepy face was distressed. "We have certain bar hours . . ."

"Right," I answered. "Understood. A man wants a drink, and some food, at dawn. Ridiculous, isn't it?"

"Yes, sir, it really is."

"Try to look at it my way. I've been up all night, working. I was brought to meet this ship by RCMP helicopter. So it's dinner time for me. On that basis, can you bring me the sandwiches, and drink?"

"I'm afraid not, sir," he replied.

"Okay, then take me to the Captain's cabin."

"Sir?"

"The captain of this bucket. I'm sure he will lend me a bottle, after he places a radio-telephone call to Vancouver."

The steward straightened his red mess jacket. He was

feeling the press of events. "Take me a few minutes, sir," he said, and in about that time was back with the food and drink, a bucket of ice, and a large bottle of club soda. I paid him in cash, adding a large tip, and he went back to wherever he had been awakened from.

I had three large drinks of the good rye, chased by soda, and ate all the sandwiches. Rinsed out the glass, washed and scoured the plate, and fell onto the bunk. When I awakened several hours later, the *Northland Prince* was slamming northward through choppy seas, toward Prince Rupert, along the inland passage.

CHAPTER SEVENTEEN

IT WAS RAINING when I went ashore at Prince Rupert. This small and melancholy port is almost up to Alaska; it is usually raining there, and the town's attractions can be covered with a single glance. Inland there is fine fishing and hunting, but Prince Rupert itself is without surprises.

I rented a Ford from Tilden's, downtown, and began driving toward Tintagel, the remote village where Gorde Ferguson, Mavis' father, lived. The highway was not bad; once clear of the swampy, depressing area around Prince Rupert, it ran along through pleasant birch, larch, and evergreen stands, and the leaves on the white-columned birches were turning to flaunting gold. I saw beaver lodges in the streams, and naked saplings they had gnawed clean of bark.

Dark mountains reared up beyond the pasture lands on all sides, their crests covered with snow. Ducks, geese, and other wildfowl were thick on the smaller streams, and I kept watching the willow groves, hoping to spot a moose, but didn't. The huge humped animals often browse there, feeding on willow branches. The rain was intermittent, and nearly freezing.

A clean land, with air that had not been breathed before.

Just before dusk, I spotted the small roadside arrow which read TINTAGEL and bumped several miles down a rutted road before I came to the village, a cluster of shacks surrounding a store and filling station. While the car was being filled with gas, I got directions to Gorde Ferguson's cabin from the Indian proprietor.

Ferguson had chosen himself a fine location. The cabin was not large, but solid-looking, and it fronted on a lake several miles long. Beyond the cabin, almost to the rocky shoreline, was a large barn with a car parked in one side of it. There did not seem to be any livestock. I honked my horn, because the old soldier-sculptor had no phone and I had not been able to announce my coming.

Nothing happened. I got out of the car and walked around the cabin in gathering darkness. The door was not locked, but there was no light inside. I was standing on the narrow porch, looking around, when I saw a canoe coming in across the lake. Through falling light. It came on silently, being paddled with long, even strokes.

When it got to shore, I was waiting there. The man sitting in it stayed still when I hauled the boat halfway out of the water.

"Colonel Ferguson?" I asked the seated figure.

"That's right."

I explained that I knew his daughter, gave him my latest name, and helped him carry his gear to the cabin. The old man had long white hair and walked with a ramrod posture, courtesy of Sandringham, long ago. He also had a string of fish which weighed eight or ten pounds, but it was growing so dark I could not tell what kind they were.

When we were inside, and he had lighted two paraffin lamps, he put a pot of coffee on the bottled-gas range. Then, at the sink, he began to gut and clean the fish, and it was odd to watch. He worked them over with great dexterity, but his head was cocked to one side and so close to the work I thought he might cut off one of his own ears.

When the fish were dressed, Ferguson left three of them on the side of the sink and took the others out to lower into a cold box with a counterweighted lid. While I watched from the doorway, he took the fish entrails and other remains out to the barn, got a small shovel, and buried them. Then he closed and latched the barn doors and walked back to the cabin.

I was still unsure of my welcome, since he had not spoken since we had entered the cabin. Now he stood staring at me, and he was as tall as I was.

"You planning to spend the night here?" he asked. His voice was abrupt, had the habit of command in it, and still held the Scottish burr of his ancestors.

"I wanted to talk to you, Colonel, not intrude."

"But you've nowhere else to go?"

"No sir."

He went over to check the coffee pot, bending over it with that close squint. "Been a soldier, haven't you?"

"Yes, sir. I was a Marine Corps officer, in War Two and Korea."

He was getting down two mugs, filling them with coffee. "You'd best spend the night. It's going to freeze before morning, with rain and maybe snow. We'll drink some whiskey and eat some fish."

"Sounds good to me, Colonel," I said.

We had the coffee, sitting around the heavy, unpainted table in the center of the cabin. It tasted fine, but when he got the full quart of Canadian Club down from the shelf, with a jug of cold water from the fridge to chase it with, that tasted better. As he opened the door of the fridge, the little light came on and I realized that he had electric power but obviously preferred the softer light of the paraffin lanterns.

We had three drinks in silence; the Colonel was not much at persiflage. Then he announced without preamble that the reason he examined everything at such close range was that he was only two days back from Vancouver. Where Dr. Colin-Smythe, the well known Canadian eye surgeon who had been trained by Castro-viejo himself, had done a corneal transplant on his one good eye.

Unemotionally, he said that he had about a 60–40 chance of keeping vision in that one eye, that the old cornea had been going out on him rapidly. I commented that Mavis had not mentioned the operation, and the old man snorted.

"Of course not. And for a very good reason. She'd have been with me down there and trailed me back up here, lugging water bottles and nostrums without end. And that noisy Malcolm brat; can't abide to have him around too long. Love him, you understand, absolute image of my father, for whom he's named, but all the same, a raucous little chap."

I told the Colonel how Malcolm had set upon me, and for the first time a smile split his craggy face and transformed it. He chuckled and nodded, and suddenly we were on a new and friendlier level. As though two victims of Malcolm's indignities had much in common. The level in the bottle dropped as we talked of old battles, cabbages and kings, wolverines and their fascination for him, and ranching in the high country of the Cariboo.

Icy rain was slatting at the cabin's double windowpanes as I told him about my assignment in Vancouver. About the alderman being hauled off the operating table and kicked to death. Of my associate who had been slowly and painfully tortured in the remote place outside of Prince Rupert. The dead taxi driver in Victoria, where Mavis and Malcolm had been used as hostages. And how his tiny wolverines carved in ivory had been used as grim appendages to the corpses.

Colonel Gorde Ferguson was a good listener. His massive head, white crowned, was turned away from even the faint light of the paraffin lamps as I related the sequence of events. When I had brought them to date and fallen silent, he nodded.

"You're in Intelligence, then?"

"Yes, sir." And when he did not answer that admission, I told him I had to find a man. Jean Belliveau-Eddie Tahsis, who had escaped from the Vancouver hospital while under police guard. Ferguson did not recognize either name. So I told him about the only other lead we had: the puzzling message scribbled in his death agony by Williamson, my agent-associate.

10 DOWNING STREET. 10 DOWNIN

The old soldier-sculptor turned his head to stare directly at me. "I know the place," he said. "I'll take you there tomorrow."

Like that. A key clicking a locked door open. I watched in amazement as Ferguson got up and began to dress. He shrugged into a lynx-lined jacket with a parka hood on it.

Came over to show me the fur lining of the hood. It was dark brown, almost black, and he said it was wolverine. Most other furs matted up, he said, when the moisture in your breath was exhaled. Wolverine fur never did that. Getting a hand torch from the rack over his bunk, he led me outside to the car and we drove back down the rutted road to the cluster of hovels at Tintagel.

The store was still open, and had a crude lunch counter on one side of it. The tables and stools were half-filled with Indians bleary-eyed drunk. Colonel Ferguson went to the phone in the corner and called a number in Williams Lake, British Columbia. Person-to-person, to a man named Andy Dunsmuir. The call went through, and Ferguson said he was bringing down a chap named Miller, a Yank, tomorrow. That Miller was on an important errand.

We would arrive at daylight, or a little after. What was needed was a good horse, saddled, with a loaded rifle on it. Handgun with holster and belt, too, with a bandolier of ammunition. Preferably .44 calibre. No, no private war, just necessary. Only the one horse, thanks. Mr. Dunsmuir must have agreed to these martial arrangements because Colonel Ferguson hung up abruptly and placed another call.

This one was to a Shorty Long, and seemed to be local. Shorty, on being fetched to the phone, was tersely instructed to arrive at Ferguson's cabin at 4:30 A.M. Like Barkis, he must have been willin' because the Colonel banged up the phone again. This done, he went to have a word of greeting with the slatternly white woman behind the counter, greeted all the stolid, intoxicated Indians individually, by name, and ordered beer all around. Their moon faces twitched with pleasure around dark bloodshot eyes.

Having fulfilled his obligations, the Colonel stalked out the door into the freezing rain, not quite sleet, and I followed him. We drove back to his cabin, but slowly, since the windshield of the rented car was frozen over and the wipers would not budge. Once inside the cabin again, we barred the door for the night and went back to work on the whiskey.

In an hour, the bottle was empty and the Colonel opened another. We talked of battles, ancient and modern, and of the bottomless swamp of Asiatic manpower which had made a mockery of American arms in South Vietnam. Of what the generals should have done at the Kasserine Pass, on Saipan, at Myitkyina, and all the other blood-drenched places. I told him how it had been to chivvy the walking and frozen wounded out of the Changjin Reservoir area in Korea, and his head was held high. Still turned away from the soft radiance of the lamps, recreating the command difficulties in a situation that severe. . . .

About midnight Colonel Gorde got up and cooked the fresh-caught fish. Dividing his attention between the smoking skillet and another of hash-browning potatoes. When he put them on the table, on platters, they were garnished with crisp watercress and sided by lemon slices. A bowl of tart wild plums went with it, and the total excellence was tamped down by more strong coffee laced with Canadian Club.

Half an hour later, I had helped the Colonel wash up and we had thrown the slight debris outside, where it would soon freeze solid. My bunk was on the other side of the room from Colonel Ferguson's; it held crisp sheets and a heavy coverlet of sheared beaver. When I told the Colonel good night, and thanks, he turned that odd myopic gaze toward me.

"You, sir, are deserving of the thanks. You kept Mavis and that oaf of a Malcolm safe. For that I am deeply indebted to you."

He turned out the paraffin lamps, and the cabin was plunged into darkness. Wearing only my shorts, I slipped under the top sheet and the cradling warmth of the beaver coverlet. The wind had mounted to almost a blizzard, and the frozen moisture in it rattled against the cabin. I had slept in many places in my life, but never in one where I felt more at home.

CHAPTER EIGHTEEN

SHORTY LONG turned out to be a weather-beaten Indian of uncertain age. He shook us awake shortly after 4:30 A.M., and while we struggled into our clothes started breakfast going. This turned out to be quite a meal: fried eggs, flapjacks, moose steaks, and sour-dough biscuits which were beautiful on the outside and doughy on the inside. I solved the latter problem by not eating the insides. Mugs of scalding coffee were gentled by considerable whiskey, and in an hour we were bouncing toward Tintagel in Shorty's new pickup, which had studded tires.

Back on the main highway, we turned toward Prince George and reached that roaring town in a rare mood of quietude. As we hummed through its deserted streets, in dawn light, Colonel Ferguson told me that more hard spirits were consumed in Prince George than anywhere else in Canada. And indeed it looked like a frontier town, although I spotted a Robo-Wash and a Colonel Sanders' Kentucky Fried Chicken Emporium.

The principal thing about Prince George, however, was the overpowering smell which saturated the town. The aroma, emanating from the numerous sawmills, was that of a million tons of rotting sauerkraut. Gorde Ferguson said that the penetrating smell came from the sulphur used in processing the timber. I was relieved when we turned south, down the Alcan Highway, toward the heart of British Columbia, the high Cariboo.

There cannot be any more beautiful upland pasturelands in the world than those of the Cariboo. The rich grasslands are framed by tremendous groves of birches, their white trunks now flaunting bright gold leaves. Lakes and ponds were everywhere, often fringed by whitish alkali rings and heavy frosts. The mountains rise on both sides of the Cariboo, and are steepest to the west, topped by heavy snow.

When we were less than thirty miles from Williams Lake, Shorty turned off west, on a small side road which was hardtopped. Ten more miles, and the pickup bumped over a cattle guard and went across an enormous pasture toward a large weathered ranchhouse. The sun was up, but its rays were broken by an overcast sky. Where it hit the ground, in bright patches, the long grass sparkled with hoarfrost.

When we stopped before the big house, Colonel Ferguson said it was headquarters for Andy Dunsmuir's ranching operations. These must have been large, because there were four dark red barns beyond the house, long equipment sheds, and a complex of holding pens and corrals. Dunsmuir himself, a stocky man in a faded straw hat, came off the porch to meet us, and we went inside to have coffee and fight off another huge breakfast.

I could hear women talking upstairs, and in the kitchen. After coffee we walked out of the house and down to the corral nearest it. A saddled horse, with a rifle canted into its saddle, was tethered there; around its saddlehorn hung a gunbelt with a Colt .44 snugged into the holster. There was no bandolier, but the belt was filled with cartridges.

While I was strapping on the gunbelt and snugging it down, so that the thong was firm around my right thigh, Colonel Ferguson stood off to one side talking to Andy Dunsmuir. He must have been trying to pay for my use of the equipment and horse, but Dunsmuir only laughed and shook his head. Then I was mounted, leaning down to shake hands with the Colonel, but the horse was a trifle frisky and had to crowhop a little before he would allow this amenity.

The Colonel said brusquely that Dunsmuir could get a message to him, if I had any further need of help, and I thanked him, nodded to Shorty Long and the rancher, and rode out of the corral. West, the way Ferguson had instructed me. There was no trail, but I could not mistake the way. I crossed by more ponds and lakes, and passed birch, laurel, and sumac groves, some of them with flaming foliage. After an hour, the pastures ran out and I had to pick my way more carefully, through rougher, climbing terrain.

The trees here were only saplings, and looked like second-growth pine. Far ahead the hills sloped upward until they became sooty blue mountains with snowy crests. That country was the Chilcotin, and there were few roads through it to the west coast. I crossed the narrow-gauge rails of the Pacific & Great Eastern Railway Line, which operates up to Prince George but has a wavelike right-of-way. Where it had been cut through the rock strata, I could see dull gleamings. There was a lot of jade in the area, but it was of poor quality.

Half an hour later, when I was beginning to think I had gone wrong somewhere, I glimpsed an open vista ahead framed by slash pine. I rode toward it slowly and found myself staring at the most astonishingly inappropriate sight I had seen in years of touring the earth's odd corners.

In the large clearing ahead, beside a small lake fed by a thirty-foot waterfall, was a hunting lodge painted in a patchwork of bright pastel colors. Smoke was pouring from one of the huge chimneys; behind the lodge were four smaller cabins, also painted in vivid colors. The decorative scheme was not orderly enough to be called psychedelic, but was more drunken Mexican, unrestrained.

A legend in letters three feet high was blazoned across the front of the lodge:

10 DOWNING STREET

Other vertical signs, also in scarlet, ran down below the gabled roof on both sides. They read:

GIVENCHY, ST. LAURENT, BALENCIAGA
WORTH, DIOR, and *BALMAIN*

With application, you can make sense out of most things, but I failed with this one. A hunting and fishing lodge, one of the few male sanctuaries left in the world. . . . Titled after the official residence of the British

Prime Minister, in London, and further embellished with the house names of the leaders in feminine *haute couture,* in Paris. The best explanation I could come up with was that someone had slipped a cog.

Dismounting, I led the horse further away from the gaudy lodge and tethered him at such a distance that his whickerings could not be heard from the lodge. Then, carrying the rifle, I moved as close as I could to the clearing without being spotted, and waited for an hour. During that time, a swarthy man who did not look like the pictures of Jean Belliveau-Eddie Tahsis, came out the back door of the lodge and went to the privy behind it. After a few minutes, he reentered the lodge.

The sun had now burned off most of the overcast and was bright on the clearing, which did not help me. Because I had to get inside the lodge without being gunned down on the approach. I had hoped that I might catch the occupant, or occupants, outside, and had considered rushing the one who had been briefly to the crapper. But it was logical to suppose that if he did have a friend, or friends, left inside the lodge, they would be covering him.

You can weigh these considerations only so long. After another half hour I snapped the safeties off the holstered pistol and the rifle, after checking their chambers to be sure of a load in firing position, and took off across the open area. Toward the back door. When I shoved the back door open, a man standing in the kitchen went diving for the rifle canted in the corner, and I shot him four times with the heavy pistol.

The first slug, in the shoulder, knocked him off his feet, but he was still scrambling. The next three shots were in the head. As I ran down the passageway toward the front of the lodge, another man had the door open and was leaving. I blew the doorknob out of his hand. Another shot at his feet brought him to a halt, and he turned with his hands held high.

This one, sallow face clamped in anger and fear, was the pigeon I sought. Eddie Tahsis, who had bought the little wolverine figures from Mavis MacPherson in Victoria. Lank hair hanging, thin mouth curved into a harsh rictus, he watched me approach and made another mistake. He tried to jump me. That effort got him a knee in the balls, and a crack over the skull with the rifle butt. Which I had still off safety and which fired, damned near shooting me in the side. Of such stupidities are obituaries made.

Tahsis was senseless, sprawled on the floor, and I picked him up and carried him to the bunk on which he had been lounging when I arrived. The disheveled bunk stank, because he had been eating and drinking in it, and obviously spilling a lot. I dumped him into the filth of his own making, found some rope in a locker across the room, and bound him securely. Not only tying his feet and hands together, but passing the rope over and through the top bunk, so that he had limited motion in any direction. Then I went back to the kitchen to check the other man, but he had less head left than the cab driver Tommy Chang had blasted from behind.

Dragging his corpse by the heels out the back door, I left him in the shadowed lee of the gabled roof. Because I did not want him in full sunshine, getting ripe too quickly. I guessed, but was only guessing, that this was the other accomplice in the attack on Alderman Atwater, the one who got away originally.

Then I went back to the long front room of the lodge and waited for Eddie Tahsis to come to. Sitting in a chair, half-facing his bunk, where I could see out the opened front door of the lodge. The métis tried to lie doggo; I saw his eyelashes flicker and close again, but only lighted a small cigar and waited. When he gave up the game, and turned his head to stare at me, I nodded.

"What you want? Why you bust in here, shooting?"

"A long story, Eddie." I took the small leather case from my jacket pocket, the one I had been given in the Vancouver headquarters of the RCMP. Assembled the needled syringe, snapped the tip off the little plastic tube, and filled the syringe carefully. Held its tip up, easing in the barrel until a drop flowered at the tip of the needle.

"This liquid is succylcholine, Eddie. Not long ago you or some friends of yours used it on a confrere of mine named Williamson, outside of Prince Rupert. You tortured him with it for days and days, until he died. Remember that?"

The swarthy, bound métis shook his head so hard in denial that the oily hair bounced around his head. "I never—" he shouted.

"When given by injection," I continued, "the effect of the drug is heightened. It results in total paralysis of the body, greatly inhibits the breathing action of the lungs. After two injections, your lungs will not function at all, for two minutes at a time. Which puts a dreadful strain on the heart. I'm going to sit here and give you injections of the stuff until you wish you were dead. That is the worst part of it, that fear of imminent death."

Tahsis threw his head wildly as I rolled back his sleeve and gave him the injection, in the forearm.

"I also have the antidote here. Which will restore you and stop the body paralysis, but I will not use it until you are ready to sing like a fucking bird. And if you fight it too hard and too long, I will simply give you an overdose, and you will be dead in a couple of minutes."

Tahsis' face contorted, and while the drug was coursing down his veins, reared as high off the pillow as he could get and spat at me. I nodded and refilled the syringe, letting him see its bubbled tip. Then I watched his bodily functions slow down, and the rigor as his muscles constricted. Finally his laborious, delayed breathing, and the motion of his eyes were the only signs of life.

It took six hours, and four optimum-dosage injections before he broke down. I do not think I would have lasted that long, because toward the last his sallow face was sweating with fear as he waited for his lungs to start bellowsing again, after two minutes of inaction. While I was preparing the fifth injection, he broke down completely, tears streaming down his dark cheeks.

I emptied the syringe, cleaned it with alcohol, dried the tip, chamber, and barrel carefully, and filled it with the antidote. His recovery took another hour, and was messy. When the paralysis started wearing off, he lost sphincter control and emptied his bowels and bladder.

The bunk smelled foul, but not a lot worse than when I had come blundering in. When he did start spilling his guts, Tahsis went all the way. Almost babbling. The name of the high contact in Vancouver and Victoria, the fellow who was financing the anti-American plot, pumping money into the discontented hippie, métis, and unemployed groups in those places. The man who had furnished the paralyzing drug to torture and finish off Williamson, our inept agent.

This same man, the money source, was also the one who had arranged the big blowoff scheduled for Victoria next Friday. On that day, Tahsis said, stringy spittle running from the corners of his slack mouth, all those in the discontented underground would surface when the Yank Secretary of State drove toward the Parliament Buildings. A thousand of them would take over the Inner Harbor of Victoria, and the Empress Hotel.

Scores more would have tickets to the visitors' gallery in the main hall of the Parliament; they would riot, toss firebombs down into the chamber, and other cadres would haul down the Canadian and British Columbian flags from the building. Run up the U.S. Stars and Stripes from all the staffs.

The statue of Sir James Douglas, shining in gold leaf on the top tower of the main Parliament building, was already mined, and would be blown off its lofty perch. The mob would uproot the towering totem poles in Thunderbird Park. The flags displayed over the entrance to the Empress Hotel would all be lowered, and U.S. flags run up on all their standards.

The *Coho,* ferryboat of the Black Ball Line to Port Angeles in the United States, would be boarded and seized before she could make her morning run. Swartz Bay would be taken over, and the incoming ferry from the mainland would be firebombed. At Nanaimo, the ferry cruiser operated by Canadian-Pacific out of Vancouver Harbor would be seized and burned. The international airport north of Victoria would be occupied, and incoming aircraft would be burned.

All in the name of the United States. I whistled when I thought of the press treatment my country would get if even half of this program was carried out. There was already a sizeable and swelling tide of resentment against

Yank ownership of most Canadian businesses, and such a sudden, violent takeover would completely destroy any chance of rational dialogue between the two countries.

When Tahsis had run down completely, I left him bound and was preparing to leave, after loading both the pistol and rifle again, when he croaked a request for water. I got him a glass from the kitchen, but laughed when he implored that I loosen his hands to drink it. Wallowing in his fouled bunk, he smelled like a gut wagon.

When I walked out the back door of the gaudy lodge, I saw that the dead man was now partially in sunlight, so I dragged his bloody-headed corpse back into full shade. The horse was restive; it had been cruel to leave him tied so tight that he could not browse, but I had not been sure about how fast I might have to leave the place. I might not have had time to fit a bridle on.

I made partial amends by letting him drink at the lake beside the lodge, and then, shaking my head in wonderment at its flamboyant legends, pointed him back through the slash pine thickets. He knew the way, and in an hour and something we rode back up to the corral behind the Dunsmuir Ranch.

CHAPTER NINETEEN

THE STOCKY RANCHER invited me back into the large living room. There, as before, in the big leather chairs we had coffee and I refused a drink. While he instructed the Chinese servant about getting the horse I had ridden cared for and stabled, I gazed at the trophy heads on his wall. Moose, elk, deer, mountain ram, a Kodiak bear, and a wolf. No wolverines. And as before, I could hear voices upstairs but met no member of his family.

Not that I blamed him. Colonel Ferguson had probably told him something of the work I did, and men on bloody errands don't make good houseguests. When I returned the rifle and gun belt, offering to clean them and pay for the expended cartridges, Andy Dunsmuir shook his head. He would have them cleaned later. What other help did I require?

I explained what had happened inside the gaudy lodge, and he nodded again. He would have the undertaker in Williams Lake pick up the corpse, holding it for the local RCMP office, and he and his men would take Eddie Tahsis to that office. What else?

I asked if I could use his phone, and he led me to a pantry off the kitchen. There I placed a person-to-person call to the commanding officer of the U.S. Coast Guard Station in Port Angeles, Washington, across the Strait of Juan de Fuca. As usual, I hooked up with a cretin first try, the duty officer, who said he could not disturb the commander in his quarters.

After sufficient bickering, I got the commander on and gave him my assignment name and two telephone numbers. One in San Francisco and the other in Washington, D.C. If he was not satisfied with the first, to call the second. Then he was to dispatch, as soon as possible, an amphibian plane to Williams Lake, British Columbia, to pick me up. Further, that I didn't know what facilities the lake had but I wanted the plane today, and there were only about four hours of light left.

The commander was shocked. "We don't operate like that," he said.

"You'd better learn to, chop-chop, or the third call will be to you from the Naval Chief of Staff's office, in Washington." And I hung up.

When I went back to sit down by Dunsmuir, the rancher was smiling but didn't comment. I could tell he didn't want me in his house any longer than necessary, so I said I would appreciate a ride into Williams Lake. He nodded, said he would drive me in himself, and went upstairs while I waited out beside the garage.

As we hummed along I tried to thank him for his help. He shrugged it off. Said, "Man, I don't know what you're doing, but Gorde Ferguson recommended you. That's all you need up in this country. . . ."

When I asked about the wild paint job on the lodge, and the far-out names on it, Dunsmuir shook his head. He told me that nine years ago a retired English officer named Roger Widdicome had bought the land from him, and built the place. Using materials hauled up from Vancouver on the toy train when he could have trucked them up for half the freight cost. At first the buildings were conventionally painted, and Widdicome had catered to parties of wealthy sportsmen from eastern Canada and the United States.

Dunsmuir did not know exactly why the operation had fallen apart after a few years, but he suspected Widdicome didn't know how to handle his native guides. At any rate, they began drinking with the rich hunters and there were several scandals. The class of client began to deteriorate until finally the place became only a remote whorehouse. Everything provided, but bring your own women. . . .

Widdicome went completely round the bend, and one day a crew of painters came up from Vancouver and put the gaudy coatings and strange legends on the lodge and cabins. A year later Widdicome had killed himself in the front room of the lodge, and for several years some estate agents in Williams Lake, acting for a Vancouver bank, had been accepting short-term rentals on the place.

An ill-starred outpost of empire, and hardly a fitting surrogate for the British Prime Minister's official residence, I thought. But so perverse are people that when news of the new murder there got out, 10 Downing Street, West, would probably ask and get, for awhile, a premium rental before the sensation died down.

Andy Dunsmuir stopped in front of a café beside a pier, in Williams Lake. We shook hands, briefly, and he drove off. Too late I remembered about the rented car at Gorde Ferguson's place, but it was paid for. And I knew the doughty Colonel would see that it got back to Fort Rupert.

Twilight was lowering across the long blue lake before the Coast Guard amphibian came up from the southwest and buzzed the lake once to warn small craft out of its landing lane. When it settled onto the water and began taxiing in, I was already moving toward it in a local fishing boat.

In three hours I was back in Victoria.

CHAPTER TWENTY

I DUMPED my bag in the front room of the apartment, and when I went back to take a leak the first thing I saw was a hat on the undisturbed bed. I went in and picked it up, because it was familiar. The shiny, flat-brimmed black matador hat Kelly Wu had worn with such laughing insouciance when we visited Vancouver's Chinatown. I shook the apartment down, but there was no other sign of her, no note, nothing.

I called the desk and asked if I had had any visitors, mail or messages. No. Walking out of the apartment, I found a pay phone and put in a call to Harrellson, the reporter on the Vancouver *Province*. He answered the first ring from the switchboard, and I asked if he knew where I could locate Kelly Wu.

"Old sport," he said, but without levity, "you've been out of touch, haven't you?"

"Yes."

"It was in my story, front-page, today. Miss Wu was kidnapped yesterday afternoon by three men when she entered her apartment. About seven o'clock. She had been working late at the office with several auditors trying to untangle the late alderman's accounts. He, or someone, seems to have cooked the books."

"Did they just take her, Bert, or was she roughed up?"

"I don't know. The apartment was ripped apart; they were looking for something before she got there."

"Unhh. You can't use it, but a hat she wore on a date with me was on my bed here when I got back twenty minutes ago . . ."

The reporter whistled, and I asked him to call my

apartment house if he heard anything on her. Just to say it was Bert, and I would get back to him on another line. That I would contact him on his home phone if I heard or found anything.

"Deal," he said, and hung up. My gut ached. I thought of the mint-new, swinging Chinese girl, and knew I had caused the snatch. I was rapidly turning into something of a frigging Typhoid Mary; everybody I came near took a fall. I am always a heavy drinker, but that night I pushed it.

CHAPTER TWENTY-ONE

I SPENT most of the next three days in a business office of the Royal Trust Company, second floor. This fiscal establishment was three blocks north of the Empress Hotel on Government Street and several desks of employees had been moved out of the large corner room so that we, by which I mean the RCMP, could take it over.

With me were two mountie photographic experts tending tripod-held cameras which ran continuously, from six in the morning until 6:00 P.M. The cameras were using zoom lenses, and were focused on the rear entrance of the most elegant import shop in Victoria. Its name was Jade City, and it was owned by a Mr. R. E. Li. During the same hours another camera team was shooting at the front entance from a building across the street over a prestigious clothier's store.

During the night hours when the import shop was ostensibly closed, a relief shift observed, without photographing, both entrances. The back end opened on the narrow walkway to Bastion Alley, an elegantly restored complex of boutiques, restaurants, and handcraft shops.

Our cameras were getting what we wanted, too, based on the information I had frightened out of Eddie Tahsis, in the Cariboo lodge. Through the shop's front entrance flowed the posh trade, but at the back it was a different story. Most of those we had photographed using that entrance had been hippies, *métis,* or dissolute-looking characters who could not have had the price of the tax on most of the expensive goods carried by Jade City.

By now we knew the employees by name and on sight. And we knew the tall, elegantly clad proprietor best of all.

He kept regular hours, and I kept them with him. Open at 10:00 in the morning, closing at 5:30 in the afternoon. I had followed him home three times to a house in the expensive Upland District of Victoria.

The first two tails bombed. He went home and did not come out again, although we kept a guard on the house all night. The third afternoon he was inside an hour, then came strolling back down the flagstoned walk in a Nanaimo sweater, walking a beautiful, jet black Samoyed dog. His walk took him four blocks, around the district's curving corners, and he led the dog down a hedged driveway beside another large house.

At the back of it was a gabled garage with four stalls, all closed. He unleashed the sporting black dog, which looked like a small Chinese temple lion frisking about, and unlocked the garage stall on the right. I was in the next yard, hidden from the house on that side by a greenhouse, and I heard him start a car and let it pre-flight, idling.

A big car, powerful, with a deep growl. When he had let it run a few minutes, he cut the ignition, came out, and locked the garage stall again. Whistling the Samoyed to heel, he leashed him again and strolled back out to the street. I waited until his footsteps had dwindled, found a gap in the hedge, and beat the garage stall lock in less than a minute. The car was a Jaguar XK several years old, but as I found when I started it briefly, perfectly tuned. I reported the location of this machine to Assistant Commissioner Henning, and it was duly recorded. His men had both Li's home and Jade City well-wired, and had been busy tailing the scruffy types who entered and left the back door of the shop.

In doing so, they had uncovered over fifty arms and explosives caches, but had not touched them. Henning assured me that the surveillance involved was not difficult. Both the hippie and *métis* groups were getting instructions in the import shop, and they all seemed to have plenty of money. At night they sat around happily making Molotov cocktails and other incendiary bombs, the hippies stoned on pot or hash, and the *métis* out of their skulls on booze.

Meanwhile, the Royal Canadian Mounted Police, who

no longer owned a horse but had lots of cars, ships, trains, and planes, kept score.

By Thursday afternoon we had a pretty good idea of how many hundreds of people were involved, in Victoria, Nanaimo, and at the ferry slips and the airport. How many arms caches they had, who was guarding them, and could conjecture pretty well into tomorrow's attempted takeover of Victoria's Inner Harbor, the parliament buildings, and the rest of the island.

All this being known, I suggested that we round them all up, and seize the caches at midnight, Thursday. Assistant Commissioner Henning was opposed, and I went to a tower suite in the Empress Hotel to argue the matter with him. As it turned out, no arguing was done; I just listened.

Henning told me that his men were at the moment defusing most of the hidden bombs. They could not expect to reach all of them, of course, because many were too near the riotously celebrating groups which had assembled and made them. Dynamite sticks, stolen from mine operations, had been replaced in these arsenals by greasy-wrapped candles of the same size and paper. The petrol in the Molotov cocktails was now water. The plastic-shaped charges had been replaced by something resembling silly putty, as dangerous as the malcontents who had intended to use them lethally.

In his office, the assistant police commissioner had mounted two large-scaled maps. One was Vancouver Island, and the other Victoria itself. Around the clock RCMP clerks pushed bright-headed pins into the maps; they represented raided and inactivated caches. But the RCMP made no arrests unless they were surprised in their defusing operations.

Henning, stroking his gray guardee moustache, said he wanted the bastards out in the open. All of them, where his men could use truncheons and riot weapons on them. That was allowed under the act which had repealed Trudeau's use of the drastic War Measures regulation.

The concept was surprising to me. Henning and his men were going to let the underground protestors come out in the open full tilt with useless weapons. The Trojan horse they counted on had been beforehand emasculated. And when all the otherwise-minded were out in the open, his men would cleanse Victoria Island of its revolutionary figures. . . .

"Commissioner," I said, "I get a faint whiff here of fascism."

He turned to stare at me, briefly. "Your opinion is your own, sir. You are entitled to it, and I will report it to Washington tomorrow. In the meantime, if you don't want to help us, get on with it. Remove yourself, so I can replace you with a dependable man."

I walked out of the suite and down the cavernous hall of the Empress Hotel. In the government liquor store just north of the Empress, I bought a bottle of Bisquit and walked back to my apartment in the Beacon Hill Park high-rise building.

There I showered, had several drinks of the cognac, and tried to ignore the telephone. I knew that I could call Mavis MacPherson, and that she would come down to the apartment if I sent a cab for her. It was a cinch; all I had to do was tell her I wanted to report on my meeting with her father, Gorde.

I didn't do it because I had already caused enough damage. Instead, I just sat slugging the cognac and watching the clock, waiting for Der Tag to begin in the garden island of British Columbia. I was still at this pursuit when the phone rang; the switchboard operator told me that someone named Bert had called me from Vancouver and requested that I return his call.

It was just past 2:00 in the morning when I walked out of the apartment building into a cold rain. I sprinted to the nearest pay booth and called Harrellson's home number. He answered immediately.

Kelly Wu, the reporter reminded me, had been forcibly removed from her apartment at about 7:00 P.M. day before yesterday. Tonight, after midnight, a Vancouver taxi driver had come to police headquarters and reported seeing a slight, unresisting figure carried from a car with British Columbian plates to a launch waiting by a Burrard Inlet dock. Three men had been supporting the figure, and at first the cruising cabbie had thought they were sailors helping a drunken shipmate back on board.

Then he had realized that the figure they carried was too small to be anything but a cabin boy. Also, a fourth man had waited in the car until the launch had pulled away at high speed. The cabbie had not been able to make out the license number because the plates were mud caked. The fact that had made him come in and report was that he had read about Kelly Wu's abduction and seen her picture in the *Province*. The three men who were carrying the unresisting figure had been Chinese. Or, as he put it to Bert Harrellson, "some kinda slopeheads . . ."

Bert gave me the dockside address where this transfer had taken place, and I scribbled it down in the dim light of the telephone booth. I thanked him, said it would be wise for him to be in his city room all afternoon as I might have something interesting. He told me his deadline for the first edition, and hung up.

I walked back to the apartment through the chilling rain, and in the lobby saw that if I hurried upstairs and fell into a dead faint I could get three hours of sleep before I had to meet Assistant Commissioner Henning at the Empress Hotel.

CHAPTER TWENTY-TWO

THE DAY DAWNED serene and cloudless over Victoria's famed Inner Harbor. The rain had stopped, and early sunlight was already burning off the damp streets. The turreted bulk of the ivy-clad Empress Hotel, the huge parliament buildings of British Columbia, were massive within their frost-jeweled lawns, and the pier of the Black Ball ferry to Port Angeles, the lacy carillon tower before the new museum, and Thunderbird Park with its towering, colorful totems were sparkling.

I was waiting in one of the southwest tower suites of the Empress with Henning and the other RCMP officers directing the operation. As I watched the traffic thicken below along Government Street, Henning was reading the urgent cablegram I had just handed him. It was from Pearsall, my chief, in Washington. It stated in the clear that Victor Li, owner of the chain of import shops across Canada, including Jade City in Victoria, had been identified as mainland China's spymaster for the entire Pacific Coast of North America.

Further, Pearsall advised me, Li was a former general in Chiang's Kuomintang armies, and had attended the war college in Moscow for foreigners at the same time as Chiang's son, Chiang Kuo. That seemed an anomaly at first glance, a spymaster with one foot in Pekin and the other in Taipeh, but deduced it meant simply that Li could call on the allegiances of both Chinese expatriate groups, in Canada, the United States, and Mexico.

Henning could not understand this, at first. Fuming, he gave me back the cablegram and said, "Is the bloke in one Chinese camp, or the other?"

I explained the advantages of the man's history, but the assistant commissioner still didn't see it.

"You mean the bloke is doubling?"

"Not necessarily, although he might be. But obviously he's got the best of both worlds, Pekin's pay and direct access to the Chinese enclaves abroad which still support the Generalissimo, Chancre Jack."

The portable switchboard in the suite was accepting readiness reports from the RCMP and Victoria police outposts. The detention vans were garaged out of sight, but ready to roll. I knew that fourteen of them had been brought across on an unscheduled ferry trip, during the night, and driven to their waiting points under cover of darkness. With them had come several hundred riot-control police officers from the Vancouver force, on the mainland.

We had known that Victor Li was the man. Eddie Tahsis had blurted out his name first, as the organizer and paymaster, in the gaudy lodge up in the Cariboo. What we had not known was that he was so highly placed an agent. Breakfast was brought to the doorway of the tower suite by hotel waiters, but was wheeled inside and served by RCMP men in plainclothes. The morning wore on slowly with the rising sun gilding the harbor.

Promptly at ten o'clock the glittering cortege of black Rolls Royces and Bentleys began converging on the main Parliament Building, discharging government officials and functionaries dressed in formal morning clothes. A group of five dark limousines swept up the front drive of the Empress Hotel, and liveried doormen jumped to attention as they loaded U.S. Secretary of State Harvey Crandall, his family, and his retinue. The first and fifth cars out from under the hotel's portico held dark-suited men who kept sweeping Government Street with their shifting glances. Across shrubbery, alleys, side streets, and roofs.

When this detachment of shining sedans turned out into Government Street, it was preceded by the motorcycle honor guard, sirens wailing. A block of this keening warning, and the cavalcade turned right, with only another block to go until it halted before the steps of the main parliament building. There Prime Minister Bennett and his cabinet were waiting in striped trousers and morning coats, to greet the Yank Secretary of State.

Watching from the tower suite, I smiled wryly at all this foofaraw. Crandall's visit was an informal one; he was only on holiday, at least ostensibly. What would his Victoria hosts have done had he been on a formal visit? Blown up the harbor?

Other people had that idea. As Crandall stepped out of the second car and shook hands with Bennett, Li's army of hippies, *métis,* and other malcontents came pouring into view. Running across the tended lawns, pouring from behind the other government buildings, debouching from cars and trucks suddenly curbed.

Below us several hundred of them poured across the Empress Hotel's car park. They halted traffic on Government Street, and a following horde came down from the north, to invade the hotel itself. I watched Henning, and he watched the scruffy, riotous mobs pouring across the lawns of government buildings. Milling in the streets. Stopping buses. Pouring into the hotel far below our high suite.

The assistant commissioner was an unflappable man. He stood staring down, receiving reports, touching his graying moustache from time to time, like an over-aged jockey rating a horse. He wanted the dissident elements fully committed before he turned his men loose on them.

"Now!" he said suddenly, turning toward the switchboard, and the orders began going out by the numbers. The scene, spread below us in bright sunshine, began to change quickly. Police and plainclothes detachments began to stream out of the parliament building. The dark-suited men in the U.S. Secretary's convoy jumped out of their cars and formed a protective cordon around the official party, sidearms drawn.

The solid-sided police vans began appearing everywhere, Klaxons two-toning briskly. They stopped at appointed stations and disgorged helmeted riot-control troops who hit the ground running. Swinging heavy truncheons, they waded into the demonstrators' roadblocks and began clubbing them senseless. Down to their knees, down flat. And as they went out, they were stacked into the waiting vans like cordwood.

A bus was overturned and set afire directly in front of the hotel. Black smoke plumed from it. High as we were, we could hear faint shrieks and howls of pain, because the perfectly prepared police forces were putting the invaders down brutally and efficiently.

What made it look so one-sided was that the demonstrators were unarmed. They thought they had brought Molotov cocktails to the encounter, but water will not ignite. Some brandished sidearms and rifles, and a few groups had automatic-fire weapons, but they would not fire. The lobby of the Empress Hotel, which had been quietly evacuated of guests half an hour before the trouble began, turned into another trap. Once they were in it, trying to take over, riot-control units came at them on the double, down the cavernous hallways.

The Black Ball ferry terminal was another ambush. The swarming hippies seized it easily, and were charging up the gangplank to the *Coho* when they were pincered by police detachments fore and aft. The bearded group which invaded Thunderbird Park to topple the giant totems actually got two small ones down before its members were overwhelmed by clubbing police. Truncheoned to their knees, they were herded into the waiting vans. A few, running for their lives, or at least unbroken heads, got away, but not many.

A smaller group, including several young girls, swarmed up the circular stairway of the carillon, gift of Holland's emigrants to western Canada. They planted their explosives up at the very top, where the organist's bench was, but the shaped charges did not go off. And there was no way out, except back down the narrow stairway. One girl jumped, and from the way her right leg folded under her on the sidewalk, I knew she had broken it. She got hustled into a detention van with all the others.

In an hour it was all over. Not only in Victoria, but according to the reports pouring to Henning through the switchboard, it was over in Nanaimo and at the international airport as well. At Nanaimo, the attempt to take the Canadian-Pacific ferry slip and railway station had failed. At the airport they had been allowed inside the terminal but had never reached the other doors. Never gotten near any of the aircraft on the tarmac outside.

The Swartz Bay ferry represented another defeat, and frustration for the dissidents. They had seized the slips, and approaching roads, easily, but on orders from Henning the incoming ferries from the mainland and all the smaller islands had simply waited offshore until he gave them clearance to enter.

By two o'clock in the afternoon over 600 of the would-be rioters and would-be bombers were being held in Victoria's police station and its armory. Several hundred more were being detained at Nanaimo and in other up-island lockups. Traffic was flowing routinely along Government Street again, and the guests of the Empress Hotel, who had been confined to their rooms during the disturbance, were being served free champagne.

I was not feeling particularly proud of my part in the operation, but remembering Assistant Commissioner Henning's terse summation of it.

In the high command-post in the Empress Hotel, he had touched his moustache once more, and commented briefly to me. "Bagged the whole bloody lot of the bahstards . . ."

"Not quite," I had answered. "You haven't got Colonel Li."

"Right," he said. "I thought you'd like to do that."

CHAPTER TWENTY-THREE

I NODDED, wondering if he knew about Kelly Wu and me sleeping together. Then decided that he certainly must, because his people had been keeping a loose tail on me ever since I had first entered his office. When I told him I wanted a short-barreled belly gun, .25 calibre, with hollow-tipped cartridges, he looked doubtful.

I could understand that. All of Canada was tightening up on weapons. Since the fiasco in Montreal, the murder-kidnapping of Minister Laporte, and the snatching of the Englishman, gun licenses to individuals were not permitted under the recently invoked War Measures Act.

"This Li is smooth, but can be rough," I added. "I don't want to try him without some firepower."

The assistant commissioner mulled it over for a few seconds, and called one of his men over. That man left the high hotel suite for the RCMP arsenal, and I waited. By the time he returned, the hotel command post had been shut down; only Henning and I were waiting. He accepted the small automatic in the clip-on holster, and asked the plainclothes officer to wait for him in the lobby.

I handed him back the holster, broke and inspected the pistol, and loaded it. The barrel was only three inches long, and you had to be close to make it hit anything, but the hollow-nosed loads did a good tearing job. Henning watched curiously as I removed my jacket and stowed the small pistol into cloth loops sewn to the inside band of my trousers, in back.

There, the little weapon was snugged into the small of my back and would not be noticed when I had my jacket on. Stowage in this location had several advantages. If you got taken, and were patted down, not many people included this spot. The weapon was much easier to draw from its supporting loops than it might have seemed, and if you were trussed with your arms behind the back, you still had a chance to get the pistol free.

"Cowboy stuff!" snorted Henning. "Be lucky if you don't shoot yourself in the bum." Adding that he would be in his office until late, he strode out with his stiff grenadier's stride. I gave him ten minutes to clear the Empress' lobby, then walked through it myself and caught a cab. To the exclusive Upland District, where colonel-importer-master spy Li lived.

He was not at home, although lights showed inside the palatial house. I had not expected him to be. I paid the cab off a block from the house and walked through the gathering darkness to the RCMP guard posted nearest me. No, Mr. Li had not returned to the house since leaving for his shop at nine o'clock that morning. The lights inside the house? Staff only: cook, maid, and gardener.

I thanked the constable and walked the four blocks to the other large house, the one with the four-car garage. The stake-out constable there challenged me sharply, flashing a torch in my face, because it was nearly full dark. No, sir, the tuned Jaguar in the locked stall had not been approached. This conversation took place on the front edge of the adjoining lawn, but so thick were the trees, shrubs, and vegetation, we could not be seen from either house.

I asked him if there was a guard on the rear of the place, and he assured me there was. Then I asked him to walk down the dark driveway with me, and while he held the torch on the lock, I beat it again. After I had slipped inside, he clicked the lock in place and faded back down the driveway to his previous place of concealment.

I got into the left-hand door, opposite the driver's side, and settled down on the worn leather upholstery. I wanted to light a small cigar after the first half hour of waiting, but didn't do it. In that enclosed space, any tobacco smoke would have lingered for hours, and been an immediate tipoff.

I sat for several hours with the little belly gun in my lap.

There was little noise outside; the streets of the Upland District were all curved, which prevented fast driving, and traffic on these suburban streets was light. Just as I was reflecting that Colonel Li had thrown me a sweeping curve, that the car was not his getaway machine after all, something scratched outside.

The lock clicked open, and the doors were swung wide. Watching the curved rearview mirror, I could see a tall figure silhouetted against the rising moon. When Li swung the right door open, my wrist was cocked upward, holding the pistol.

"Good evening, Colonel," I said as he sank to the seat beside me. "Don't move suddenly, please, or I'll blow your head off."

He sat still, with both his hands in view. A languid, elegant-looking man with a sword-blade Manchu profile.

"Where's Kelly Wu?" I asked.

"I couldn't say, really." Li sighed. With my gun aimed at his head the bastard actually sighed. And the upper-crust Mayfair accent sounded strange, coming from him, but it was authentic. "Or perhaps we could do a deal. She's alive. If I tell you where, will you call off these RCMP dogs and give me running room?"

I stared at him, and told a lie. "Yes," I answered. "I will make that deal. Now ease out slowly with your hands away from your body, and meet me at the back of the car. Agreed?"

"Yes." He slipped out of the car, and I moved with him, out the other door. I knew there would be at least a second, when the curved top of the Jaguar intervened, when I would have him out of the line of fire. I was prepared to risk that fleeting second. My decision was wrong.

As he straightened up, his left hand shot downward to the walnut instrument panel, snapped a knob, and the tuned Jaguar exploded. The outer doors of the garage were blown off, I was slammed against the side wall, and as I lost consciousness, realized that I was hemorrhaging from both ears. . . .

CHAPTER TWENTY-FOUR

I SEEMED to be spiraling up out of a darkened tunnel, with increasing speed, toward blinding light. My ears ached, but when I reached for them, I could not move my hands. They were pinioned. I opened my eyes, and the bright light was intolerable. A taste of copper salts was in my mouth, and I needed water badly . . .

Slowly, as my eyes focused, I realized that I was in a hospital room. A white-coated doctor was bending over me, light flashing off the mirrored ring strapped to his forehead. A nurse stood behind him. I lowered my gaze and saw, at the edge of dimness, Henning, the RCMP chief, standing at the foot of my bed. I jerked at my hands again, but they would not move. I was under restraint.

The leaning doctor snapped off his forehead light, and straightened "Don't jerk, please," he advised me in a wind-tunnel voice. "You want to claw your ears, but we can't have that."

I tried to tell him, mouthing the words like cotton candy, that the left eardrum had been ruptured before. Plane crash, in Burma.

He seemed not to hear. First in one ear, then the other, used a little aerosol bottle to dust in a white powder. Straightening, he snapped off his little headband light, and spoke patiently over my head.

"The powder is a mix of neomycin–polymyxin and boric acid. There are perforations on both sides, but we will make no attempt to remove the blood clots. If you follow the prescribed regimen, stay quiet, keep the ears dry, spontaneous closure of the perforations may occur. I saw the older wound in the left ear; it is greatly enlarged now and might cause trouble."

He turned, instructing the nurse who was taking down

his words like holy writ. Arrogant bastards, these doctors. . . . I was just two bad ears to this one, nothing more.

Wheeling, the two white-coated dispensers of mercy left the room briskly, and Henning moved around to take their place. When I batted my eyes toward the water carafe, he filled a glass with the lovely stuff, tinkling with ice, and put a curved plastic straw into it.

I drank deeply while he held the glass for me. Like a Bedouin pedestrian who had been a long time between oases. Some of the cotton candy dissolved, and I managed a more intelligible croak.

"Extent of injuries?"

"Providentially, just the ruptured eardrums. A little hide lost, here and there . . ."

"Colonel Li?"

"Dead. Force of the explosion seems to have been mostly on his side of the car. Flying hardware in the chest and head."

I considered this drowsily, realizing that I was heavily sedated.

"He said . . . Kelly Wu was still alive. Offered a deal. Any news?"

"No." Henning shook his head in regret.

"How long will I be here?"

"Several days, they say. Old man, I'm very sorry about this. Perhaps we didn't do—"

"What I'm paid for, Commissioner. Will you inform Neal Pearsall, Washington office, of the Agency?"

"Right away. Anything else?"

"Yes, sir. I'd like a phone put in here, my hands released, and the latest editions of the papers, both Victoria and Vancouver, sent up."

He nodded. "Try my best. Thing about freeing the hands depends on the doctor, of course. See you in the morning."

I nodded, and he went stalking out. I was beginning to feel fond of the brusque bastard, which is a poor way to run a railroad. But then railroads are largely out of style, anyway. In a few minutes a disapproving nurse came in with several newspapers and released my wrists from bondage. I blew her a kiss with both hands, and she huffed out again.

CHAPTER TWENTY-FIVE

IN ANOTHER HOUR, I was sedated again and the pain in the ears had dwindled to a dull aching. Holding the receiver well away from the right one, I dialed the hospital switchboard and placed a call to Bert Harrellson, in the *Province* city room. The reporter was not at his desk, so I left word for him to call back. He did, in half an hour. When he was set, I roughed in the events which had led to the highly efficient and brutal putting down of the attempted takeover on Vancouver Island.

Twice during the narration I had to caution him to speak low, because when he raised his voice the sound lanced at my perforated tympanic membranes. I cautioned that he was not to mention me in any way, and that he was to lay it on for Assistant Commissioner Henning, who had really planned the operation. That Colonel Li was dead, killed in a booby-trapped car, but nothing more of that incident. Finally, that he was not to put the story through without Henning's okay. I thought he could get it approved quickly.

Harrellson thanked me, said he had heard nothing more about the pretty Chinese girl. I did not tell him that she was Colonel Li's niece, and that he had told me a few seconds before his death that she was still alive.

"That's it, then?" he asked. "You'll be leaving soon?"

"I expect so. But wait a minute . . ." I read him off the number in the center of the telephone dial, with my extension, and said I would be there a couple of days, if he heard anything.

"Right. Thanks again. . . ." He rang off, and I read the local and mainland newspapers until the print started blurring on me. Switching off the light groggily, I dropped into a hard, opiate sleep.

I was having breakfast the next morning when Harrellson called back.

"Man, why didn't you tell me you were in hospital?"

"Nothing serious, Bert. No reason to."

"I'll bet. I ran across something by accident which may mean nothing, but I thought you ought to know. The *Dong Feng,* a mainland Chinese freighter, left here early yesterday. Her announced destination was Canton; she carried general cargo, and was berthed at the CP pier close to where Miss Wu was last seen. Or some person who may have been Kelly. You follow?"

"Right on," I answered. Excitement, and conjecture flickered. Kelly had pointed out the white Chinese freighter on our first midnight stroll.

"Okay," Bert went on. "I used to cover the harbor for the paper, and I automatically glance at the *Arrivals & Departures, Ships in Harbor* charts. The one in the Victoria *Times* this morning announces that the *Dong Feng* is tied up at a berth in the Inner Harbor."

I was silent, smoking the news over. The ship had turned up in time to take Colonel Li aboard, for one thing, if his takeover had succeeded, or even if there had been an appreciable island riot. What better place to conceal the abducted Chinese girl, if she was to be a last-resort pawn, in case he got into trouble . . .

"Are you there?" asked Bert impatiently.

"Yes. It's interesting, and I'll check it out. Right away."

"I'll be here," answered Harrellson, and clicked off.

Before I had finished dressing there was quite a crowd in my room. The chief of nurses, the intern on duty, and the resident. We bickered with some heat, and I allowed them to blow the dust into my ears again. Then I held up both hands, said that I was aware of the dire possibilities involved in further trauma to my ears. But that I had heard so much crap in my life that it might be soothing to be totally deaf.

When I walked out and down the hall, they were muttering behind me. Henning was in his office and didn't seem overjoyed to see me, so I knew they had phoned him. *Whole thing was a bad show, really.*

I agreed, saying that life was mostly sorrow brought on largely by ignorant chaps like me. Then I told him about the *Dong Feng,* and said I wanted to go aboard it with the search party he was about to send. He bridled at this direct approach, mentioning Canada's economic contacts with mainland China, by which he meant the lucrative grain shipments.

I didn't answer that, since I was beginning to understand Henning. He was a law-and-order man, certainly, subject to all the political winds, but he was also that rare thing, a gentleman. A man with decent instincts. I let him run on. *Quite out of the question, main problem of the dissidents already solved, sorry about Miss Wu, of course, etc.*

When he was through with his discourse, he picked up a phone, called the Victoria harbor master, and said he wanted an immediate report, by return call, on why the Chinese freighter was tied up in the Inner Harbor when her destination from Vancouver had been announced as Canton, in the People's Republic of China?

His inquiry was softly spoken, but held the hint of barbed wire. In an hour the harbor master called back. The *Dong Feng* had left Vancouver routinely, but midway across the Georgia Strait had cabled a deviation to Victoria. Trouble developing in her main-shaft housing. She had tied up at ten o'clock yesterday morning in the Inner Harbor, behind the CP Princess cruise ships, laid up for the season.

The harbor master said he was getting on to the shipyards and repair people, and would call back. Henning hung up, not looking enthusiastic. He said we would wait to hear the details, of course, but that he could not board a foreign vessel without more evidence of some wrongdoing.

"She's on the ship," I insisted. "Li offered me the trade, saying she was still alive. But he's dead now, and her value as a hostage is gone. They've got to kill her quick, to clear themselves . . ."

He was staring at me stonily, tanned and weathered

hands steepled before his sandy gray moustache, when the phone rang again.

"Yes? Henning here. Go ahead, Captain." And he listened while I watched him listen. Once he threw his head aside, as if he had bitten into a quince, but kept on listening and murmuring. Finally he said "thanks," listened another minute. Asked the harbor captain to send him, immediately, anything which would familiarize his men with the Chinese freighter's layout, both hull and superstructure.

Also, he wanted at least five of the regular customs inspectors for the port to join his search party, which would board the *Dong Feng* in an hour. Possible? Yes, even if they had to delay the search of other vessels. After hanging up again, he leaned back in his chair and stared at me.

"Sir," he said, "it is my honest hope that you will leave this country soon, and never return except on holiday. It seems that I must order the search party, indeed I have just ordered part of it. The *Dong Feng* did complain of excessive vibration in her main-shaft housing, but she has not requested any repair services. She has been at her berth now . . ." He glanced at his watch. ". . . for twenty-four hours with power on her main diesel.

"In addition, there is no evidence of any repair work being carried on aboard her. She has hoisted the departure-from-port pennant, and ordered a pilot to come aboard in two hours. So we'll have a look."

CHAPTER TWENTY-SIX

ON THE WAY to the *Dong Feng*'s berth, in Henning's dark, unmarked sedan, we studied the blueprints on the ship. She was 10,100 deadweight tons; her hull and superstructure had been turned out by Howaldstwerke, Hamburg A. G. She was powered by a main diesel engine turning up 11,650 horsepower at 118 revolutions per minute. This engine had been furnished by the Motorenwerken Augsburg Nuernburg, and she also carried auxiliary power plants of four Deutz diesels, 500 horsepower apiece, and on an upper tween deck, an 112 horse docking diesel.

Five hatches, number three with reefer refrigerated sections. The *Dong Feng* had been in service for eight years, and her runs out of Canton alternated between Vancouver and Auckland, New Zealand. She could not accommodate containerized cargo below decks, but often carried the large metal boxes on her main deck, stowed beside MacGregor sliding hatches.

There were twenty in the search party, including the five diverted customs inspectors. They were waiting in the open-sided warehouse beside the Chinese freighter, and the rest of us arrived in four cars and went on board immediately. Everybody but myself fanned out by prearrangement, Assistant Commissioner Henning going directly to the Captain's quarters to serve the warrant.

I wandered into the ship's lounge and dining room–bar, and found it spotless but without decoration except for plastic flowers in wall brackets. No one opposed our entry. When I climbed up to the bridge deck, the Chinese seaman and officer on duty there glanced at me but did not speak. They both wore neatly laundered uniforms without insignia, and it was only from their positions in the wheel house that I could tell their rank.

I walked through, out the starboard side doorway, and climbed up to the "monkey island," or observation deck, just above the wheelhouse. Nobody was there, and I stood watching Henning's men and the customs inspectors swarm over both the forward and aft decks. The MacGregor hatches went sliding back, and part of the search party went down into them to check around the general cargo wedged by nylon pillows and slabs.

When I went below again to the sterile lounge–bar salon, Henning was using it as a command post. The sullen Chinese Captain sat beside him, listening to the RCMP and customs men reporting. After an hour, it became apparent that they weren't going to turn up anything. They had been into the paint locker, at the aft end of the freighter, checked all crews and officers quarters, and did what they could in the five hatches.

There was a hoarse blast, near the ship, and it nearly ripped my head apart. The last of the customs inspectors came in to report that no one was secreted in the 150-foot-long tunnel over the main shaft, and Henning turned toward me.

"The pilot's ready to come aboard," he explained. "The ship is ready to clear this harbor unless I can find a reason to hold it. And I can find none."

I nodded wearily, and winced when the hoarse whistle blasted again.

"I appreciate the effort, sir," I said. And I meant it. Henning went up to the bridge deck with the sullen Captain. I heard his crisp voice racketing out over the speakers on the decks, advising all his people to go ashore immediately.

They did, trooping obediently down the gangplank. Which was soon rattled upward and stowed against the shoreward rail. Commands in Chinese began booming through the ship's speaker. Be ready to cast off the forward and aft lines; wait for the order. The freighter was ready to depart; her decks quickened with increased power on the main diesel.

I could hear it all clearly, even in the darkness of the paint locker. The *Dong Feng*'s gangplank was up. The pilot was aboard, and she was moving away from the pier.

CHAPTER TWENTY-SEVEN

THE PAINT LOCKER, because of its high combustibility, was well ventilated, but I knew I had better climb out as soon as possible. Sitting on one of the stacked five-gallon cans, I felt the ship shudder as she moved away from her mooring. What I had in mind was fairly suicidal; I meant to search the Chinese freighter again, because I was sure Kelly Wu was on it.

True, it had just been gone over carefully by Henning, his men, and the customs inspectors, but they had had only an hour. And a ship of ten thousand tons has so many hiding places that there is only one way to do it properly: there must be several hundred men and they must invade, simultaneously, every hatch, the upper decks and superstructure, and the engine room.

What chance had I? First, I had the elements of surprise and secrecy, and I had more time. All the way to Canton, if my luck held. This last is a joke. I could not possibly go undetected for more than a day, with seamen moving around the ship on routine errands. And I had a flashlight, but no weapon, and a fair knowledge of the ship's construction.

Now, while the Chinese freighter was being conned out of the Inner Harbor by the pilot, was the best time to start. Those in the ship's company who didn't have duties to perform would be at her rails, staring back at the last port they would see before mainland China.

Climbing up the companionway ladder from the paint locker, I glanced around cautiously. Two Chinese seamen were leaning on the rail watching Victoria Harbor diminish. I moved silently behind them to the companionway, to the steering flat, where I swiftly inspected the rudder control–motor room. Number 6 hatch was next and I dropped down only far enough to see that the little laddered hallway was empty. The vegetable oil tanks were nearly full, and if Kelly Wu had been dropped into one of them, it was too late anyway.

There was a noise above, on the main deck, and without hesitating I went dropping down the steel ladder. All the way to the emergency entrance, to the propellor-shaft tunnel. This tunnel was tall enough for me to stand upright; it ran beside the massive, glistening length of the swiftly revolving shaft. The tunnel was brightly lighted and therefore very dangerous for me.

Hurrying through it toward the engine room, I stopped short of the emergency bulkhead door, which was open. My ears began to ache, so near the throbbing, nine-pistoned monster of a diesel, but I had no time to worry about them. On the far side of the engine room, his back to me, was a Chinese engineering officer; his hands were on the main engine control handwheel. He was staring at the dials before him. The only other man I could see was a wiper, working at the far end of the giant diesel.

My only way out was up the engine-room stairway, and it made two turns before it reached the main deck. Taking a firm grip on the flashlight, I waited until the wiper had worked his way around the far end of the diesel bed; then I went sprinting toward the steel stairway and up to it. Sprinting, but cautiously, because there was a thin film of oil on everything.

The lights of the engine room glittered off the hand rails and rungs, and the controlled power driving the shaft shook everything I touched. One more flight of stairs, a straight shot to the deck opening. I was only a few feet from it when a Chinese seaman stepped out on the ladder above me. He wore khaki shorts, a short-sleeved singlet of the same material, and a look of astonishment.

I muttered "don't block the way, fool!" in what I hoped was Cantonese. When he nodded hastily and stepped aside, I wheeled and bladed him across the throat with the rigid outer parts of my hands. Bones cracked in his neck, and I put one shoulder under him as he collapsed. He didn't weigh much.

Stepping out on the main deck, I turned right and ran, crouching and taking him along, to the companionway leading to number three hatch. It was, fortunately, so close to the rising superstructure that I was not visible from the bridge deck. When I was safe inside the top platform of that stairwell, I dumped him with relief.

He may not have weighed much, but he smelled high: of rice wine, raw sweat, and the engine room. There was a small stowage chamber opening off the stairwell, and after clipping him twice more, I dumped him into it, and latched the metal door.

Hatch three was all reefer chambers for frozen meat. Moving faster now, because if I hadn't killed the engine-room seaman, he would recover consciousness and begin hammering on the door and walls of the locker. Or his failure to report for duty would be noticed. I searched "A" deck of the hatch. The chill air blasted at me; the thermometer inside the access door read "three degrees centigrade."

Whole carcasses of beef and pork hung from hooks, swinging slightly from the motion of the moving ship. Grayish, their fat solidified, the floorboards down between the carcasses slick with both ice and frozen drippings.

"B" deck, just below, was the same. I searched down the lines of slaughtered and dressed hanging animals with care. But the cold was beginning to get to me, and before I dropped down the companionway ladder to the next level, I had to flail my arms and dance in place, restoring circulation.

"C" deck presented a new problem. Here the frozen carcasses were not hung, but stacked. There were access lanes between them too, kept free by nylon wedges which allowed the carcasses to shift without damage, but they were harder to check. I spent twice as long in that reefer chamber as I had in the upper two, and when I came out had to redouble my dancing and flailing.

I found her in the lower hold. The refrigerated chamber next to the *Dong Feng*'s double-bottom. She was at the very back of it, naked and wrapped in a tarpaulin. Kneeling beside her slight figure, I started to remove the chilled tarp, and then decided it might take skin off with it. Gathering her up, I went back out to the bottom of the laddered well and lowered her gently.

Kelly Wu's lovely ivory skin was marbled; she appeared to be dead. I listened for respiratory sounds, against her icy lips and cold breast, but could hear none. Then I tried the pulse in her stiff right wrist, and felt an incredible rush of thanks when I detected a faint pulse. It was thready and uneven, but her heart was beating.

Carefully removing the tarp, inch by inch, I threw it aside and lifted her in my arms. Held her against the warmth of my own body as I had done before, in a happier time. I do not know how long we stayed clasped like that. It might have been half an hour, because although I was worried about the seaman I had knocked out and his alerting the crew, I also knew that only warmth would bring the chilled girl back to life. And Kelly Wu had been a friend of mine, prodigal with her own warmth.

When she moaned, and I felt her move for the first time, I wrapped her in my shirt, jacket, and trousers, covering the petite body as well as I could. And that was nearly all, because she couldn't have weighed much over 110 pounds, tall as she was. After this divesting of vestments, I was left in my shorts and shoes, holding a flashlight.

I went up the steel stairway, grabbing rungs with one hand and holding the flashlight in the other. When I reached the top of the wellhead, I had an acute problem. I was nearly naked, had only the flashlight, and had to get forward, to the stairway aft of the superstructure. In broad daylight, on a working ship.

A chancy proposition, surely. But I was like that ant trying to shift the rubber tree; I had high hopes. I went haring out of the companionway entrance, down the roofed way on the starboard side of the main deck. A Chinese deckhand had the bad fortune to be drinking from the metal fountain at the aft end of the superstructure. He glanced around at me, slanted eyes widening at the sight of a foreign devil in his drawers. I hit him so hard with the flashlight that it bent in the middle.

Up the short stairway to the next deck, wheeling past a lifeboat to another stairway. The bridge deck. The seaman on watch at the starboard wing gaped as I went winging up to "monkey island," the observation deck. As I stepped out onto it I saw him break toward the wheelhouse, and knew that I had precious few minutes, or seconds, before I was surrounded and captured. But, in prowling this "monkey island" beforehand, I had planned the possibilities. Running straight to the locker which held the pennants, flags, and flares, I grabbed one of the flare pistols and triggered it almost straight up.

The shell it hurled aloft was for daytime use. At the height of its trajectory it ejected an orange smokebomb on a small parachute. The bright stain spread over the bright afternoon sky, above the choppy blue Pacific waters. When the Chinese crew members came piling up the ladders to the observation deck, I stood them off for awhile by firing the rest of the parachute flares at them, point blank.

That killed enough time. Four harbor launches from Victoria which had been trailing us closed with a rush, their sirens keening. There was one tense moment when the *Dong Feng* refused to reduce her power, even after they had cautioned her through their hailers. A bow-gun shot from the lead launch smashed through the wheelhouse windows, and the Chinese freighter's power went off abruptly. She began losing way in the choppy waters.

Cursing the crewmen who held me, in Chinese, I shrugged free and went to the housing which held the ship's own electronic hailer. My voice, brazenly amplified, echoed across the water as I informed Henning that I had found Miss Wu. That she was near death from freezing. That I would bring her to the port rail, main deck, so that one of the launches could get her to hospital as quickly as possible.

Even before the launch's response came, I was pushing through the sullen Chinese crewmen, hurrying down the ladders two rungs at a time. I brought Kelly back up the companionway ladder of number three hatch over my shoulder. She seemed more limber, but was still moaning.

While Commissioner Henning stood in the wheelhouse

with a service automatic pointed at the Chinese Captain's head, her body was lowered in a sling to the launch pitching below. I was there to receive it. And to hold her clasped against me as before, while the launch swerved away from the Chinese freighter and headed back to Victoria with its motors roaring at capacity. Up on the step, pounding across the wave-chop.

CHAPTER TWENTY-EIGHT

BY TEN O'CLOCK that night, Kelly Wu was out of danger. Her doctor, the same bad-tempered one who had treated my ears, said that she could not have been in the refrigerated chamber longer than several hours. That she had obviously been held somewhere else on the ship, and transferred to the reefer. She had been chilled long enough to develop a severe edema in the right foot and calf, and the tips of two of her fingers on the left hand seemed to be necrotic.

It had not been necessary to debride any skin, the tired young doctor said, but if they could not halt the necrosis two of the fingertips would have to be amputated. He seemed personally affronted by the trauma I had brought into his hospital: first, me with shattered ears, and then the pretty Chinese girl mistreated and frozen almost to an icicle.

"I don't know what you damned people are doing," he complained, "but I wish to Christ you'd stop it. I have to make out those frigging police reports when I'm supposed to be sleeping . . ."

I nodded solemnly, glad that he hadn't handled the assault on the alderman while he was in surgery and I had cranked up the Pier Six brawl. Still bitching bitterly, he took me down to the hospital pharmacy and got me a bottle of aerosol antibiotic. Said to use it three times a day, keeping my ears dry, and stomped off without accepting any payment.

From the apartment, I called Mr. Harold Wu, Kelly's father, at his home. After I had given him a quick brief on the matter, skipping most of it, he thanked me gravely in sing-song but dignified English. I replied that she had gotten into trouble because of me, and that I was therefore obligated to do all I could. And had been fortunate . . .

He asked me to call Kelly and tell her that they, he and the mother, would be over to see her on the early morning ferry. So I dialed the hospital, but its switchboard stayed busy, and finally I fell across the bed and slept with my clothes on.

CHAPTER TWENTY-NINE

"RUN AROUND . . . *And run around . . . Been in this old town too long . . .*"

I was humming the jump tune softly, and Mavis MacPherson turned to stare at me. In inquiry. When I shrugged, she turned back to watch the little river in the forested valley, just below us. It was late afternoon, and we were sitting in a battered station wagon she had borrowed, watching thousands and thousands of coho salmon trying to fight their way up the river.

They weren't making it; there wasn't enough water. The homing fish had been roiling at the river's entrance for days, trying to fight their way up what was only a trickle, to their spawning grounds. The Goldstream River is ten miles west of Victoria, on Vancouver Island, and the salmon have been returning there since before the white man came.

This year, there had been an extended drouth all over the island. We watched their thick, dull-silvered bodies jostle and ram each other. The females were sluggish, heavy with roe. If they did not get enough water to fight upstream, they would release the roe where they were and the milky eggs would be discharged fruitlessly in the tidal waters and surf.

The packed salmon were already weary from a long sea pilgrimage, and scaly with parasites. Wheeling clouds of gulls, ospreys, and other hawks were dive-bombing them, screaming harshly, plucking out their eyes with beaks and talons. . . .

Mavis had told me on the drive out that impounded lake waters in the mountains above served both Victoria

city and the Goldstream River. The annual salmon ru
could be saved if the city authorities would release wate
into the river for only a few days. But, fearing a late
shortage which would prevent watering Victoria's famou
gardens, the city fathers had not agreed to this.

So the fish were dying. Clogging the narrow stream
bruising each other, prey to the plummeting birds.
cursed the city fathers and their famous flower gardens
and asked Mavis to drive me to the airport. She started th
station wagon without comment, and drove back towar
town through a thundery twilight.

Earlier in the afternoon, I had said goodbye to her ram
bunctious young son, Malcolm. He had ignored my hand
characteristically, and taken a parting punch at me. Prop
erly appalled that his beautiful blond mother was takin
me someplace, and leaving *him* behind.

"I had a letter from Dad about you," commente
Mavis. And I knew no power on earth could keep he
from telling me what the nearly blind old soldier–sculpto
had written in the letter. The short skirt had ridden hig
on her shapely thighs, and I could smell the womanl
smell of her. Not perfume; the oils of sweat, and desire
with a trace of frustration, too.

"He said you were a man wound tight, fit to ride th
High Cariboo with . . ."

I grunted. I was seeing his massive white head lifte
again, in the lonely cabin up north of Tintagel, with freez
ing rain slatting on its walls . . .

You couldn't stop the woman's mouth. "I had writte
him before, what you said about every man uncovering
when a holder of the Victoria Cross walked down th
street."

"Whissht!" I said sharply. "Aren't you the bigmouth
He liked me well enough because I helped you and hi
grandson, and because I had been a soldier once. Got sho
at, and hit."

She was smiling, the shapely bitch. We did not speak
again until she stopped before the small airport building
in gathering darkness. When I turned to reach for my bag
on the seat behind, she pulled my head down.

I endured it, my head against her breast.

"You're a wild man, skinned and raw, like a flighty horse spooked by dust devils. Stay a week with us, for bed and breakfast, and more. Then you might want to stay another week. Besides, Malcolm has never really had a good shot at you. I could bring him in some night, while you slept, and he could black your eye properly."

I laughed at that, and lifted my head. He'd do it, too. Got my bag, and swung it and myself out of the old station wagon. The door wouldn't latch properly; I had to slam it twice. Then leaned down.

"Get married to a man with proper hours and prospects," I instructed her. "You are all I ever thought a woman could be. There aren't many like you around. And Malcolm needs a man around fulltime, to build a boot factory in his butt . . ."

Mavis nodded, brushing a strand of the tawny hair aside. She was not crying, and not smiling. "You're the man I want," she said. "I'll be here, waiting to hear from you."

She started the old borrowed car, and drove away from the airport terminal. I walked inside it, checked my bag at the Pacific Western counter, and sat down on a bench, waiting for my plane to arrive.

I wanted the woman badly, and could have arranged a few weeks, or longer, in the town. Malcolm had always filled me with secret glee, because the obstreperous young boy was what we had called in my youth "a going Jessie." I thought of standing surrogate for him against the ills and misadventures of small boys trying to puzzle out a world in which they are often lonely and helpless . . . Of the deep peace with Mavis in the master bedroom's double bed, with Malcolm burrowing between us.

She would wait, she had said. How long do you wait on an irregular man who cannot even tell you where he works? While I watched, the twilight lengthened over Vancouver Island, and the runway lights flashed on.